ALISTAIR

Golden Streak Series
Book 2

By

KATHI S. BARTON

World Castle Publishing, LLC

This is a work of fiction. Names, characters, places, and incidents are products of the author's imagination or are used fictitiously and are not to be construed as real. Any resemblance to actual events, locations, organizations, or person, living or dead, is entirely coincidental.

WCP

World Castle Publishing, LLC
Pensacola, Florida

Copyright © Kathi S. Barton 2013
ISBN: 9781939865700
First Edition World Castle Publishing, LLC July 22, 2013
http://www.worldcastlepublishing.com

Cover: Karen Fuller
Photos: Shutterstock
Editor: Eric R. Johnston

CHAPTER 1

Alistair knew that, whatever happened with this client, he was going to go on a long vacation and not take his cell phone with him. This was the stupidest person he'd ever taken on. He stood up when the judge entered the room, and tried to jerk his client up. He really needed this like he needed a hole in his head.

"Your client is asleep, Alistair. Have you become so boring that you have to drag them from their beds to give yourself something to do?" The judge, Thomas Gilbert, a good friend, laughed. "You can still take my place, if you want."

"No thanks. I think Ryland would murder me in my bed." He looked down at the man snoring loudly beside him. "You think we can just get this finished while he's out? It might go a little bit easier if I don't have to explain everything to him twice."

Thomas nodded and picked up the file the bailiff had handed him. He looked it over quickly, then asked Alistair what the game plan was. His client was in for driving drunk on a sidewalk and through a mall. It was pretty much open and shut, but the guy had called in a favor from Brock, and as much as Brock had hated to ask, Alistair was representing the man.

"I don't suppose we could put him in jail for thirty and forget about him." Thomas laughed, as did the bailiff at his request. "Fine and time served?"

"All right, but he's gonna have to come help with the cleanup, too. Nearly took out the taco place with his drunken behavior, and you know how much I love those suckers." The gavel came down hard, but the man didn't stir. It wasn't until he was being lifted by the two police officers that he woke enough to ask what was going on.

Alistair didn't bother trying to reply, even as the guy was screaming at him to explain what the fuck was happening. As Alistair closed up his brief case, he tossed his coat over his arm and headed out. Plans for some time off were already forming in his head as he moved toward the back of the courtroom and out to what he hoped was freedom. He nodded to the officer who opened the door for him, and froze in place as the officer dropped to the floor with a bullet in his head.

The screaming made him duck behind the door he'd nearly stepped out from behind. Thomas was shouting something from behind him, but Alistair couldn't hear him over the din in the hall. He could hear shots being fired and moved further back from the door as someone fired one off near the room he was in. The man who entered looked at him and pointed the gun right at his head.

"Get the fuck up." Alistair nodded and stood, keeping his hands up. "Come here. You're going to make a nice shield for me when I get out of here. Things didn't go like I planned them and now…well…."

Alistair didn't argue but did as he was told. He felt his brother touch his mind and told him to wait because he was in danger.

"What the fuck do you mean wait? I can feel your terror now. Something has happened and either you tell me or I'm coming down there now."

Alistair was being held close to the man behind him, and begged Ryland to stay away. *"You'll only get yourself killed, and your wife will kill me if you do."* He took a deep breath as they moved into the hall and Alistair got his first look around. *"I'm being held with a gun to my head to be, as he put it, a shield. Call for help but stay away, please. I can see seven bodies in front of me, and I don't want to see you among them. Please, Ryland, listen to me for once."*

"All right, I won't come into the court house but I'm fucking coming to you. I'm on the phone with the police now, and they want to know which floor you're on and if you know who's holding you."

"I don't fucking know him. We've not had a chance to exchange email addresses yet, but as soon as we do, I'll make sure you're the first to know. Christ, is everyone stupid today?" Ryland laughed, which made Alistair feel less tense as well. *"I don't know him. He's about six-four, two hundred and fifty pounds, tats over his face and neck. I think one of them is a tear drop."*

"All right, I've told them. They said to hang tight...whatever the fuck that means." Alistair didn't know either, but planned on hanging onto his life if possible. *"Don't get yourself killed, all right?"* Alistair told him he'd try not to.

A cop stepped in front of them told them to halt, and when his captor laughed, Alistair didn't have to look to see that he was going to kill him. The gun went off so close to his ear that he felt his ear drum pound. The young cop dropped as if his feet were taken from under him. Alistair told Ryland the name that he'd seen on his name badge.

The man holding him stopped moving forward and Alistair knew that he was going to be shot next. He could hear the cops coming in and barking orders for everyone to lie down. This was not going to end well, and he told his brother that. He opened his eyes, only just realizing that he'd closed them when the man behind him spoke. There was a lovely woman standing in front of them, and she looked as terrified as Alistair felt.

"You want I should shoot you?" The woman shook her head and held up her hands. "Then you best be getting out of my way. I got what I came for and you're going to be another bullet point if you don't get the fuck back."

"You came for him?" Confused, Alistair looked around and realized she was talking about him. "I hope the fuck he's worth it. Is he your lover or something?"

"No, he ain't my lover. What the fuck is wrong with you?" He pointed the gun at her and tightened his grip around Alistair's throat. "I said to get the fuck back. I got no real cause to kill you, but that don't mean I won't if you push me."

"Okay. Okay. I just wanted to…." She looked around, then back at them as she took a step forward. "You do know that you're not going to get out of here alive, right? That man you have in front of you won't offer you much protection once the guys outside shoot him up a bit."

Alistair wanted to snarl at her, but he couldn't talk. "What the fuck do you care for, anyway? He your lover or something? He just don't look like your type. You should be with a more manly man. Like me."

"Christ, no. I mean no, he's not my lover, either. He's not my type. I like my men a little less legal. No, I was asking because you really seem like a man that has a plan and I was wondering if I could tag along when you leave. I'm here for…robbery, and I don't want any jail time, either." She took another step forward, then a second one. Alistair didn't think the man noticed. Just what he needed, he thought, the two of them holding him as body armor.

"You think to come along with me outta here? I got me a car waiting. I only came in to kill off the cocksucker that got me into prison the first time. He ain't gonna be sending anyone up again."

The girl nodded and took another step. She was about five feet from them now. "That's cool." The girl nodded and looked at him. "I don't suppose you checked him for weapons, did you? I mean, I know there are laws and all, but you never know about these legal asses. They do think they're above the law."

"Shit. Didn't think of that. He might have something on him right now." The guy nodded at her, nearly taking his head off as he looked at her again. "You come on over here and check him out. Don't do anything stupid, because I'll blow your fucking brains out too. I don't need a woman who don't obey when she should. You mind me and we'll get out of here just fine and dandy."

She nodded as she took the last two steps between them. Alistair watched her move slowly and felt her place her hands on his chest, then run them down along his ribs. He felt her breath on his cheek as she leaned into him, and he wanted to nip at her flesh. She looked up at the man who was holding him.

"I can't check his back. You have him too tight against you for me to look there. You think you could let him go enough that I can feel down his back? I'm betting he has something there. I would hate for us to get out the door and he pulls something out and shoots one of us."

The man loosened his grip just a little and her hands slid behind him and along his back, but only for a second. He felt her jerk suddenly as the man holding him moved. Then the gun went off. Alistair felt his air rush back into his lungs quickly when he was let go, but it wasn't until he fell on the floor that he realized that the woman had tossed him to the side. She staggered back, and Alistair noticed the knife in the chest of his captor. She'd killed him. He looked at the girl as she took another step back. He started to go to her, not sure what had happened, when she turned to him and he saw the blood.

"He shot you," he said. She looked at him and pulled her hand away from her waist. Her hand was covered in blood. As he moved toward her, she took several more steps back until she hit the wall behind her.

"Don't touch me." He stopped moving toward her when she leaned back against the wall. "You hurt?"

"No. Let me help you." He started forward again and saw the gun. "You won't shoot me. You just saved me. Let me help you."

"I have to go and rest a minute." He thought she meant that she had to sit, but when she moved toward the stairs instead, he started for her again. "You come any closer, I'll shoot you. I swear to Christ you can't be that stupid."

"I'm not, but you are if you think I'm going to let you walk out of here."

The door to the front of the courthouse burst open and he looked toward it. Several men were coming in, all of them armed and in full gear. He looked back toward the woman. She was gone. Drops of blood left a trail and he started for them, but stopped when he was told to stand still.

Raising his hands over his head, he told the cops who he was, and that a woman who had helped him had been shot.

"She's gone that way." He nodded to the blood on the floor. Then he was tossed down, and his entire body searched in seconds. It was as thorough as any exam he'd had at a doctor's office. Then he was cuffed. "You have to help her. She saved my life."

"We'll get to her in a minute. Right now, we're going to see who you are and ask you a few questions. There's been a shooting, and there are people dead."

No shit.

Alistair tried to remain still as they searched him again and then asked him what had happened. He told them quickly, and asked again if they could find the girl. One of the men nodded and took off toward the stairwell where her blood trail had gone. Alistair was uncuffed almost immediately, but he wasn't let go for another hour.

Alistair was escorted from the building with two others that had apparently passed whatever test the men inside were conducting. The killer was dead, and Alistair understood that there might be a second killer, but he would have thought to get everyone out, not set them up like bowling pins in a long alley. His brothers were there, and he held them off when they tried to hug him. He explained quickly what had happened, tore off the part of his shirt that she'd touched, and handed it to them.

"You have to find her. She saved my life, and without her I'd be in the next body bag that comes out." Each of them took off in different directions except for Ryland, who said he was staying with him.

"Mom knows you were in the building. She's called me four times. When I told her that I could see you, she said for me to stay with you until she could see you herself. And Bronwyn is coming down as well."

Great. His mom and his pregnant sister-in-law. He went to the ambulance to be checked out and waited to hear from one of his brothers. *She couldn't have gotten that far with a bleeding belly, could she?*

An hour later, each of his brothers came back without any information on the girl. Brock said he had smelled her in the halls but had lost her in the crowds of people that came and went in there daily.

"She could be living in the building for all we know, but she didn't come out. And there is no sign that she was with the man, not if what you say is true about her killing him." Alistair had been watching the gurneys as they came out and knew that Brock was right. "I'll see what I can find out at the hospital. Sindy is working tonight. Maybe she knows."

Sindy Wilson was a friend of his family, and a nurse at the hospital. If anyone came in, she'd find them, because she was just like them—a tiger. Alistair waited for his turn to talk to the police again, this time in a room that had been set up for that purpose, and watched as his friend Thomas was brought out. He'd been shot once in the head, too. The police he'd been asked to speak to were dazed and seemed to be overwhelmed. Alistair knew just how they felt. He told them everything that had happened, including how the girl had saved him.

"You think she was with him?" Alistair frowned at the officer. "She had a knife in a building that strictly says 'no weapons.' Could they have been together is all I'm asking you."

"I'm pretty sure that a gun is a weapon, as well, and the stupid prick that held me had one of those pointed right at my head when she stabbed him in the fucking chest. How do you suppose we should prosecute him? To the full extent of the law? Have him put in the chair? Oh wait, he's already dead.

Moron." He took a deep breath, trying to control his temper and his cat. "Look. He didn't seem to know her at all. When she appeared in front of us he seemed just as surprised by it as I was. He even threatened to kill her if she didn't get out of the way. She saved my life, and I would very much like it if you found her. As I've said several times, she was injured and is in need of medical attention."

They nodded…twice, as a matter of fact. Then they asked him to be available if they had any more questions. He left the room they'd set up for questioning and went down the hall to the bathroom and tore off his jacket, then pulled his t-shirt over his head.

"You going somewhere, big brother?" He felt Brock speak to him and tried to ignore him. *"I'm standing right outside the door, so when you come out, you'd better be dressed and ready to come home or there will be hell to pay. Not to mention there are about fifty cops running around this building looking for something to shoot. I'm pretty sure a tiger will make their day."*

Alistair leaned his head against the stall door. *"She's out there fucking hurt and not one of those idiots is going to look for her."*

"True, but that doesn't mean we won't. Just that we can't right now. I'm working on getting me and someone else into the building after they all leave. You think Keith might want to join me?" Alistair snarled at his brother. *"Yeah, I thought so. Just hang tight and let me fix this. We'll find her if she's in here."*

"You think she is, too?" Brock told him he was sure of it. She hadn't been found, so it meant that she'd either left already or was still inside.

"We'll find her." Alistair felt better already. He came out of the men's room and walked with his brother down the hall

and out of the building. Neither of them was stopped, as they moved with confidence.

Brock told him what he'd planned already. It was a good, solid plan, but when Alistair asked how they would get her out if she was there, he heard Brock laugh. Alistair didn't find any of this the least bit funny.

"I'm still working on it. I have a plan to get us in to look. One step at a time." They were outside again when Brock asked him why he needed to find her so badly.

"I don't know. She saved me. Isn't that enough?" Brock nodded at his lie, both of them knowing what it was. "Besides, this is the second time I've nearly been shot by someone and a woman has saved me. Maybe next time she'll be my mate, and I can retire a happy man because I'll have my own protector."

Brock snorted and told him he should be so lucky. By the time everyone left, they had a plan not only to get in, but to get her out if they found her. Alistair watched from the diner across the street as the last light went out and the police started making their rounds around the outside perimeter. When Brock stood, so did Alistair.

"My way, right?" Alistair nodded. "And the first sign that she's armed or doesn't want to come with us we leave her. I'm serious about this, Alistair. I'm not going to drag a woman out that doesn't want to be found."

"Agreed. But if she's not conscious, then we bring her out anyway and take her to the hospital." Brock nodded this time. "Brock, what if she's dead already?"

"Then we go to plan b." He walked away before Alistair could ask him what that plan was, and he was pretty sure he didn't want to know. If she was dead, then…then he had no clue. But she wouldn't be. He didn't know why he was so sure of that, but he was certain she was still alive. His very future depended on it.

~~~

Ally let the water boil for ten minutes before she took it off the hotplate. She dropped the needle and thread into it and looked at the wound again. Christ, what the fuck had she been thinking? Leaning back, she closed her eyes. When she could take out the needle, she would try and stitch herself up, but in the mean time she thought about what she'd done. Murder was something she hadn't planned on.

The man had already shot five people before she'd come up the stairs, and before she could think to get out, he'd killed four more as she watched in horror; he simply aimed and pulled the trigger. She'd only stepped out of her hidey-hole to save the cop, but he'd been shot before she could help him. Then the man had seen her and she knew that she was going to die, too.

The gun in his hand had terrified her, but she was more afraid for the man he held in his arms. When she'd started forward to try and talk him out of killing him she'd known the moment he pointed the gun at her that she was going to have to kill or be killed. Might as well become less of a statistic and more of a hero, she'd thought when she told him she'd help.

Closing her eyes, she knew that if she had to do it all over again she would have.

Someone cleared their throat and she jerked up.

"I'm not going to hurt you." She looked at the man standing there in the shadows and thought for sure it was the man's partner coming back for revenge. "We've been looking for you to see how badly you're hurt. I swear we aren't here to hurt you at all."

"I'm fine," she said. Then she realized what he'd said. "We? Did you come with Lance? Did he...?"

She started gathering her things quickly, stuffing them into her duffle, uncaring now what they looked like. If Lance was there, she needed to get out right fucking now. The man called for someone named Alistair, but she knew that Lance couldn't be far behind. When she had all she thought she could reasonably carry, she moved back against the wall again, but another man stood there.

"I'm not going with you. I don't care how much he's paid you. I won't go." The second man nodded as he moved toward her. "Stay back. I have a...I've got a gun."

"No you don't, and we're not taking you to anyone named Lance. I'm the man from today, the one you saved." He moved into the light from her lantern. "My name is Alistair Golden, and this is my brother, Brock."

"I don't care who you are. I said to stay back." She started moving toward the back of the room where she knew there was another door. She'd made sure she had two ways out if something like this ever happened. And she was glad now that she'd taken the time to scope the place out so she knew just how many steps it was to the door.

"I'm sorry, miss, but I can't let you stay here. Not now. You'll have to come with us, and we'll make sure you have proper care and are safe from Lance." She laughed, knowing it sounded manic. "You don't believe me?"

"No." She glanced to her right and knew that she'd have to run if she wanted to make it before he got to her. When she turned back, he was nearly on top of her. She cringed when he raised his hand.

"I won't hurt you," he said.

She whimpered, unable to stop it.

"I swear to you I won't hurt you. Let me help you."

"Please, just leave me alone. I saved you." She slid down the wall and curled into a tight ball, finding comfort in the old habit. "I saved you. Leave me alone."

"Alistair, we have to go. I've got her things…just pick her up and let's get out of here before someone comes along." She felt his hands on her shoulders and she kicked out at him. She wasn't going back, and no one was going to make her.

When he lifted her up, she fought to get away. She wasn't any good at fighting back, but she was going to try her best. He cussed when she slammed her fist into his mouth, but she was certain it'd hurt her more. As she nursed her hand, he threw her over his shoulder. And the slap to her ass made her still.

"You want us all to go to jail? If not, I suggest you please be quiet. This isn't exactly legal, you know." They turned and she whimpered again. His shoulder was digging into her wound. "Is this all you have?"

She didn't answer, but the other man picked up her duffel. Then they were plunged into darkness.

"Please. I'll do anything you want. Anything. Just don't take me back to him. I'm begging you. I swear to you if you take me back he'll hurt me…maybe kill me. Is that what you'd do to someone who saved your life?"

"The only place you're going is my house." She heard the anger in his voice, but the man behind them laughed. "This isn't fucking funny. I'm trying to be the good guy here and I feel like a shit."

The man laughed harder. "How's that working out for you? From where I'm standing, you have a woman on your shoulder that's going to knock the shit out of you or both of us as soon as you put her down. And it's doubtful that she's going to keep quiet enough for us to get out of here without alerting the entire police department. And did you think to check her wound before you threw her on your shoulder, caveman? I smell blood and it's fresh."

The man started cussing again. She struggled, but when he adjusted her, she blacked out. Her last thought was that Lance was going to be thrilled to death to have her back. And she was reasonably sure he wasn't going to throw her a party.

CHAPTER 2

Alistair watched Sindy stitch the woman's wound up. It wasn't as bad as he'd thought it had been. Just an in and out, she'd called it. The bullet had entered in the fleshy part of her waist and exited the same way, leaving a long, open wound. When she was putting the last of the tape on the gauze, she turned to him.

"You do know that she's not going to be happy when she wakes, don't you? And from what Brock told me, she's going to try and get out of here the first chance she gets. Are you aware that she's running from someone? I'm betting it's a husband." Alistair nodded. "What's the plan?"

"I don't know." He sat down and looked at the woman on the bed, then at his friend. "She's my mate."

He'd thought she was yesterday when she saved him. Then when he stood over her last night, he'd known for sure. Alistair looked at Sindy when she laughed. He wasn't amused.

"You Golden men sure do know how to pick them, don't you?" She pulled the sheet up over the woman and started picking up the things she'd brought with her. "I would say from what you told me about her that she's been abused. Badly too, if the scars are any indication, and there are some

15

that are very deep, but nothing fresh. I'd say the newest ones are three to six months old. It looks like he might have taken a belt to her and used the buckle end on her a few times. Dana used to do the same to me when the mood struck him."

Sindy had been given to a man who nearly killed her on a weekly, if not daily, basis. And when he wasn't trying to kill her, he raped her repeatedly. She had only survived because her best friend and Ryland, his brother's mate, had killed him.

"Have you told your brothers yet?" He shook his head. "I'd make it quick if I were you. Whoever is chasing her is going to find her, and you know how pissy Ryland gets when things don't go his way."

"I heard that." They both looked at the doorway when Ryland walked through it. "Brock said you found her. I'm glad for you. She looks like she might make it. Why did you bring her here and not the hospital? I'm assuming you have a good reason for bringing a human here."

He nodded, more depressed than he'd ever been for some reason. "She's my mate. And she's married. She mentioned a man named Lance when we went to get her, and that she didn't want to go back to him. She said she'd do anything not to. I think I might know who he is."

Ryland sat down but didn't say anything. Alistair was trying to work out how to protect someone that didn't really belong to him but to another...and the irony of it all. He wasn't coming up with any answers.

When Bronwyn walked in, she took one look at him, then walked to the bed and touched the girl's forehead. "Her name is Ally...no, Allyson Isaac. Her husband is...." She looked at him and he nodded. "You know him."

"Sort of. I know of him, not him. He's a big time lawyer in DC that has been in the papers a great deal lately. Mostly, he's been talking about his case, and had mentioned that his wife is away resting at some resort. He claims that the miscarriage she had a few months back depressed her to the point where he thought she'd be better off getting professional help. He mostly talks about himself and his progress in the case he was working on."

"I didn't have a miscarriage. I wasn't ever pregnant by him…thank God. He's a monster to me. I can't think what he'd do to a little baby," the woman said. Alistair jumped when Allyson spoke. "I'd like my things so I can leave now before he finds out where I am. Unless, of course, you've already told him. Have you?"

"No. I told you that I wouldn't harm you, and if that means keeping you from him, then that's what I'll do. He won't know you're here." Alistair moved to the bed and wanted to reach for her, but didn't. "How long have you been running?"

She sat up slowly, and Bronwyn helped her. She didn't answer him, and he really wasn't surprised by that. When she asked again for her things, Alistair asked for Ryland and Bronwyn to give him a few minutes. They walked out the door, but Ryland turned to her before leaving them.

"This man that's chasing you, did he hurt you? Is that why you left him?" She nodded, not having any choice but to answer him because of the amount of compulsion he'd put into his voice. "Then he's as good as dead if he comes here to get you."

She watched him leave, and when the door closed behind him, she looked at Alistair. "He really thinks that he can just kill him? Just like that? Who are you people?"

Alistair didn't answer her but moved toward her slowly. "I'm Alistair Golden. You and I met last night. I'm sorry I hurt you, but getting you out was important to me. Are you in any pain right now?"

"I know who you are. Another lawyer just like him. And more than likely rich, too." She started opening drawers and then the closet before she turned to him again. "Where are my things? I know they have to be here somewhere."

He felt his body respond to the way she was dressed. He'd given Sindy one of his shirts to put on her when she'd had to cut away the one Ally was wearing. Alistair just hadn't realized that she'd taken off her pants, too. And the way Ally was standing now, with the light behind her, made him realize that she had no bra on either.

"I put them in the laundry. The housekeeper said she'd wash them and bring them up when they're clean. I think she said it would take an hour." He sat down before he lost the battle to take her into his arms. "You'll be safer here than in the basement of the courthouse, and as I said before, Lance won't find you here."

"He'll know because you bastards always talk. And having me will be like icing on a cake for you, I'm sure. I'm not going back to him. If he owes you money or you've got a big case coming up against him and plan to use me as leverage, I got news for you. I won't go easily."

"No, I doubt you would. If that were my plan. But as I've told you several times already, I'm not going to give you to him. I'll keep you safe." She snorted. "Are you always this trusting of people who try to help you?"

"I didn't ask for your *help*." She said *help* like it was something nasty. "And yes, I'm an equal opportunity distruster, so don't think you're all that special." He felt his temper rise.

"Look, I said I'd help you, and I will. Now get back in that bed and stop dancing around this room dressed like that." He flushed when she glared at him. "I'm seriously trying my best not to bend you over my knee and beat that lovely ass of yours."

"You wouldn't dare." It was a challenge, and he knew it. As he stepped toward her to do just as he'd threatened, he heard the door open behind him. He turned, shoving her behind him, and growled low.

His mom froze. He couldn't move for several seconds until his cat calmed. His anger and the need to protect his mate had nearly made him shift. His mom smiled and brought the tray she had in her hands to the table he used as a desk when he needed it.

"Hello. You must be starved. My name is Sandra Golden, I'm his mom. Come on, have some lunch." When neither of them moved, his mom came over and touched his arm gently, and then moved him out of the way to get to Allyson. "Come along, dear, and have something to eat. It'll help you to deal with overbearing men."

"I don't want anything." His mom nodded but pushed her into the chair anyway. "Seriously, I'm not hungry. I have to get dressed before someone beats my ass, and then find another place to hide."

Allyson's belly rumbled, and she flushed. His mom handed her the fork and told her to eat and not to be silly. She sat across from her, and Alistair sat on the bed. It already smelled like her.

"I think you should know that this house, like all the houses that my sons own, is very well secured. Of course, Jules lives in an apartment building, but it seems secure enough. Ryland mentioned that you were running from an abusive man. Good for you." Allyson looked up at his mom as she continued. "Men who hurt others should be shot in the dick if you ask me."

KATHI S. BARTON

Alistair burst out laughing, and Allyson started coughing. He went to her to see if he could help, sure that she'd choked on a piece of lettuce. She waved him away and stared at his mom.

"Do you normally say what you think like that?" His mom shrugged at Allyson's question. "I can't. I try, but it normally comes out as incoherent babble. Or I have a really good comeback when they are gone."

"My daughter, Bronwyn—I think you've met her—she says you should have two comebacks ready at all times. Then, you can say them without thinking about it. One of hers is…." She looked at Alistair, bringing him into the conversation. "What is it she says?"

"I'm going to shoot you in the foot. She claims that she doesn't really think she'll do it, but she is ready to if need be." He sat at the table with them, having moved off the bed. "My mother is trying to come up with one that will involve both a male and female situation. As you've heard, she has the male one down pat."

Allyson nodded. They talked to her while she ate. She was eating the last bite of pie when she looked at the empty plates. She looked embarrassed.

"I guess I was hungrier than I thought. I don't usually get a meal like this one where I live now." His mom gathered up the plates. "If you could show me where I can find my clothes, I can be on my way."

His mom patted her hand and left, closing the door behind her. Allyson turned to him and glared. He raised his brow at her.

"If you think because your mom is nice that I'm going to suddenly trust you, you're as loony as they come." He laughed. "I don't think this is the least bit funny. You're to bring me my clothes right now."

"No. But it's bullshit what you said about not being able to say what you think. You've had no problems whatsoever telling me exactly what you think." He stood up again, reached for the day's paper, and handed it to her. "They're running your prints off the knife. Will they find yours in the system?"

She took the paper from him and stared at it. There was a large picture of the courthouse after all the police and ambulances had shown up. She looked up at him, and he could see tears in her eyes. She nodded slowly.

"A few months after we married, Lance had me register for a gun permit. I never got a gun, but I did take all the classes because he said it would be good for his image. I would imagine that they keep those on record." He nodded. "I wished so many times that I had gotten a gun."

He didn't say anything about her teary confession, but sat down across from her again. He waited while she cried for a few minutes before he spoke to her. She was going to have to trust him now. And he was sure that once she heard what he had to tell her, she wasn't going to.

"They'll figure out who you are, but not where you are. Brock and I took all your belongings from the basement, but we didn't think to check for prints or any DNA. If someone wants to, they'll be able to figure out where you've been staying. I don't know why they would, but someone could. How long had you been staying there?"

"Twenty-seven days. I never stay in a place more than thirty…sometimes less, but never more. I was in an abandoned warehouse before that, and over the garage of a house that had been foreclosed on before that." She got up to pace, and he watched her. "I'll need my things more now that they'll find my prints. I have to get out of here. He'll find out where I am quicker now. And my money. If you took my bags, you had to know I had some money stashed away."

He stood up, went to the bedside table, opened the drawer, and nodded to the things there. She didn't take it out but stared at it. She had to know it wouldn't get her far enough this time.

"He'll know you're here as soon as it hits the paper that your prints were on the knife that killed that man. And the two hundred dollars you have here won't get you far. He'll be on you before you could get to another state. They'll put your picture in the paper, and I would imagine he would offer a reward. He'll get you if you leave here." He wanted to pull her into his arms, but didn't. She still didn't trust him.

"I have to do something. I can't just sit here and wait for him to come and drag me back home." She laughed bitterly. "I think I'd prefer jail time over staying with him. Especially after this time. He's not going to be terribly happy with me if he gets me back. I just might not survive if I do go back."

"You've left him before." She nodded at his statement. "How long were you gone before he brought you back?"

"Which time?" She sat on the bed. "I have no idea why you want to know this. I just…I'm so tired of running. I've left him and been brought back so many times I can't think beyond just the last few times. I can't…you have no idea what sort of asshole he is."

She sat there with her eyes closed, and he watched her. Tears began to fall, and he felt his heart constrict. She was his mate and she was hurting. It didn't seem to matter that they hadn't bonded yet, but when she hurt, he wanted to fix it.

"My mother said he'd be a good catch. I never cared for him, but my mom liked him. I suppose I did, too, at first, but when he hit me the first time, I should have known that he was going to continue. Instead of calling off the wedding, I went ahead and married him, thinking that I could simply leave if he ever did it again." She laughed again. "I tried to leave him a month after we were married. Fat lot of good that did me. He'd backhanded me because I said his tie didn't match his shirt."

"Christ." Before he could talk himself out of it, he went to the bed and sat down next to her. Pulling her into his arms had been chancy, but when she didn't fight him, he held her to his chest. He could smell her fear and her resignation at the situation.

"After that, every day was a war. The cook tried to defend me once, and he ended up in an accident on his way to work one morning. He died three days later. Then the maid that helped me dress every day begged me to leave him, and she'd disappeared a few days later. She'd seen all the bruises and had figured out what they meant, I suppose, and he didn't much care for anyone else knowing *his business,* as he called it. After that, there was no more domestic help in the house. Not that it mattered. He made me do it all anyway. But the violence got worse, and I could no longer hide the truth from others, especially my mom."

"Did he hurt her?" She nodded. "Is she dead, too?" He wasn't sure why he needed to know other than to see how far the man would go to keep her in line. When she didn't answer, he looked down at her and realized she was asleep. Stress won out every time, and he knew it.

Alistair reached for Bronwyn. *"I need your help. I hate to ask you this, but can you do me a huge favor?"*

"I'm not sleeping with you. You're a nice man and all, but your mate is right there. Make love to her." She laughed. *"If you want me to read her mind and find out some information, I've already gotten about all I can from her. She's led a very dangerous and oftentimes painful life. And so*

you know, she's in your arms now because I put her there. You have to get her to trust you, and I think you touching her gently is the only way. Don't fuck this up, or so help me, I'll tear your balls off and feed them to you."

Laughing, he told her thanks, but he wasn't sure this was right. He wanted Allyson to trust him because she did trust him, not because she'd been manipulated into doing so. He felt his own eyes drift shut, and got up before she woke and found him in bed with her. He had a feeling she'd not be too happy about it.

He met his brother Brock and Ryland downstairs in the kitchen. They were already reading the paper. Bronwyn was making hot tea.

"She's not married, either." He looked at her. "Allyson got a divorce from the abusive prick about two years ago when she disappeared from the golden cage he keeps her in. The judge granted it on the grounds of spousal abuse, then he helped her run. She's been about half a step ahead of Lance since. She thinks her ex is telling most people that she's in an asylum since her mom passed away and that she's resting. But Allyson doesn't think anyone believes him."

"They know he's been beating her." Bronwyn nodded, and then set a cup of tea in front of him. He just looked at it; he hated hot tea. "Why the fuck didn't any of them help her?"

"He's a lawyer with a lot of pull and heavy fists." He looked up at Allyson when she spoke. He'd not heard her come into the room. He got up, and she sat down. She was pale, and he pushed the cup of tea at her and smiled at Bronwyn, who shrugged.

"So, he uses his supposed power to keep you in line." Allyson nodded at Brock. "A man who, instead of using love, uses his fists to get what he wants. No doubt he is a bully in the courtroom, too. He sounds like a real peach. I can't wait to tangle with him."

"You can't. I mean, he'll hurt you. Not just with his fists, but…." She looked around the room, frowning. "Why are you doing this? Why are you acting like you care one fig what happens to me? I'm not in your social circles; not even Lance could be. You guys are rich beyond anything he could ever be. Not to mention well respected. Lance hasn't had anyone respect him since he graduated from kindergarten. Maybe before that."

"Having money does not give you a license to hurt others. Nor does the lack of sense make it right." Alistair leaned against the counter and watched her. "You have no reason to trust us or even believe us, but none of us will let anything happen to you. Not now."

"Why not now?" It was a good question but one he couldn't answer for her…not with his family there. He nodded to his brothers and sister as they got up to leave. Allyson sat very still as each of them hugged her gently on their way out the door. She repeated her question when the door closed.

"You have a right to know, and I want to tell you, but I've never told this to anyone who didn't have the least bit of knowledge of what we were before." He took a deep breath. "I'm a weretiger. As are the rest of my family. Bronwyn is a little more, but she can shift, too."

She didn't move or say anything, making him nervous. He watched her closely for any signs of freaking out, and when she stood up, so did he. She poured the last of her tea into the sink and turned to leave the kitchen. She stopped at the door.

"If you didn't want to tell me, that's fine, but making fun of me isn't nice." He was confused. "I don't appreciate you going through my things to find ways to put me down. I got enough of that from Lance the entire time we were married. You could simply have said you wanted to fuck me, but that outlandish story was cruel."

He tried to think what was in her things and went to the laundry room to find her bag after she left the room. Deep in the bottom were five books, all of them about the paranormal, and all of them romance. Two of them were about cats: one a panther, the other a tiger. He put them back in the bag and tried to think of how to fix this. He picked up the books again and went to find her. Proving to her what he'd said was true was going to take a lot of trust. He just hoped she didn't really have a gun on her.

By the time he got to the bedroom door, he'd unbuttoned his shirt. He knocked sharply once, and when she didn't answer, he opened it anyway. She was putting her things into one of the empty bags that had been in the trashcan.

"Sit down, please." She continued pulling the small things out of the little drawer. "I would very much like it if you would sit down. And whatever you do, don't run. I like to chase things. It's in my nature, and if you run, I might hurt you."

She snorted. "So much for you telling me you won't hurt me. Get out until I'm finished packing, and I want my other things, too. I don't care if they're soaking wet."

He pulled off his shirt and dropped it on the floor. Then he toed off his shoes and unbuckled his belt. She turned to watch him, and he could feel her fear. He knew that as soon as he shifted she was going to run and he was going to chase her. That scared him and excited his cat.

Pulling off his pants but leaving his boxers on, he let his cat take him. He moaned as he pulled him under, and welcomed the change from human to cat. He blinked several times to get her to come into focus. She stood very still for several seconds before she screamed.

Then, like he knew she would, she ran.

CHAPTER 3

There was nowhere for her to go. She pressed herself as tightly as she could against the wall and tried not to think about what had just happened. When he moved toward her, she put up her hand, not having a clue what the heck she was going to do to stop him from eating her alive.

"Stay back." He moved toward her. She moved along the wall to get away from him. She could see the door and wondered if she could make it when he growled. Her entire body felt it, and she had a moment of wondering why it felt as if he'd stroked her.

The closer she got to the door the closer he got to her. It wasn't until he was only about two feet from her that she realized how big he was...not just big, but *fucking huge*. Nothing she'd ever seen in the zoo or even on the television had come close to how big he was. When she touched the doorknob, he growled again, and she tore it open and ran. As soon as she was down the long hallway and almost to the stairs she fell forward with him at her back.

"Please don't kill me. Please, don't. Please." She tried to crawl away, but he held her down with his weight. She could hardly breathe, much less move. When he licked along her bare shoulder, she shivered, knowing that at any second he was going to bite her. When he licked her again, she realized he was tasting her.

"Stop that right now." She rolled over and smacked him on the nose. "You're licking me like I'm a tasty steak, and I'm not."

He snorted at her and laid his massive head down on her chest. She tried to wiggle out from under him, but he lifted his paws up and put them on either side of her. She was trapped.

She looked into his eyes and tried not to think about this thing being a tiger. She was looking for Alistair. When he blinked at her, she could have sworn he smiled, but his teeth were a little too close and too large for her to think that's what he was doing.

"Are you really a cat? I mean, I can see that you are but…are you going to eat me?" He stilled over her, and she had the most erotic thought pop into her head. She squirmed to get out from under him. "I didn't mean that the way it sounded."

The more she struggled, the more thoughts popped into her head. She stopped and looked up at him. She had no idea why, but she thought he was doing it.

"Can you read my mind?" He shook his head. "But you can…according to the books I've read. I know that they're just romance, but you can speak to me through this link thing. Can you do that?"

He licked her again, and she had a feeling he was trying to tell her something. She waited, trying to think what had happened in the books. When it occurred to her, she looked at him wide-eyed.

"You can't think you're going to bite me, right?" He nodded, and she felt faint. "You'll take my arm off if you do that. I don't think…do you think you could become a man again? This is very one sided."

She felt the tightening of the air around them, and suddenly, Alistair was over her where the cat had been. She wasn't sure this was any better and told him so.

"For me it is." He shifted his body, and she felt him settle between her legs. She could also feel that he was hard. Honestly, she wasn't sure if she wanted him to move off her or to do some of the things she'd seen in her mind just a few minutes before.

"You have to get off me. This is very uncomfortable." He nuzzled against her neck, and she moaned. "You need to stop that right now."

"I will. But you brought up communication. I can nip you here and you'll be able to talk to me whenever you want."

When he ran his tongue along her throat, she could think of a great many things she wanted to say to him, and not many of them were about communication. When he nipped gently at her throat, she moaned and ran her fingers up the back of his neck to his hair. She jerked him hard up and off her.

"Not nice, love. I was beginning to get the taste of you in my mouth. By the way, you smell like sex." She shivered at his tone and his words, and pulled him up again when he started licking her again. "You do know that I'm naked, don't you? And every time you wiggle under me, I'm getting harder. Very hard, in fact."

That made her stop trying to move from under him. He was naked, and now that he said it, she felt his hand move up her thigh to her hip. He was going to touch her, and she couldn't make herself fight him. She wasn't even sure that she wanted to any more.

"The thought of you laying here with nothing but panties and my shirt on has me thinking all sorts of thoughts. Like how wet are you? I can smell your arousal, and it's calling to me. I would love to slide into you. Take you slowly and hear you scream my name." Her fingers were no longer holding him back, and he seemed to know it as he moved back to her throat, then her mouth. His mouth feathered over hers back and forth before he suckled her lower lip into his mouth and nibbled on her.

Her mind was telling her to stop this madness, that she couldn't trust him, but her body was telling her to open her thighs wider and let him take her. When his mouth moved down her throat to her shoulder, he rolled his hips into her. When he rubbed his chin over her breast, her breath caught, and she moaned, curling her fingers into his hair as he took her nipple into his mouth. Then, he bit her.

"Please. You have to...I think." Her body was on fire, and he was the only thing that could put out the flame. He lifted his head and watched her as he reached into the collar of the shirt she had on and tore it down, exposing her breast. He lowered his head and suckled on the hard tip, all the while watching her. And when he opened his mouth wider, he took in as much flesh as he could. She rolled up her hips to meet his thrusts.

"Come for me, Allyson. Come and let me smell your scent." He moved again and tore away her panties. She felt his naked cock at her entrance and felt herself get wetter. She lifted her legs to wrap around him as he slid into her. She cried out from the pleasure and begged for more.

~~~

He'd only meant to tease her into a climax, bring her to it, and then move away. But now that he was inside her, all he could think to do was claim her, make her come with him as he bit her. He rolled to his back and brought her with him, and she sat up over him. Reaching up, he tore her shirt off completely and pulled her over him to show her how to ride him.

Her body was beautiful. As he pulled her hips forward, she moaned and began to do as he wanted her to, her movement making her breasts, full and tight, sway slightly. Sitting up, he took one into his mouth while he toyed and played with the other. She was riding him harder, faster now, and he rolled her to her back again and held her hands above her head as he settled tightly inside of her.

"I want to mark you." She nodded and begged him to finish her. "When I bite you, you'll be mine. Do you understand what that means?"

"I don't care. Please, you have to help me come. I'm so close that I can't think." He moved into her deeper, knowing that on some level what he was doing—what they were doing—was wrong, but this cat wanted her, too.

When he let her arms go, she wrapped them around him and pulled him tighter. His balls were so full and close to his body that he knew the moment she had her release he was going to follow her. Licking a path from her nipple to her throat, then to her shoulder, she tightened around him, and he knew she was coming. When she screamed, her body gripping his, he sank his canines into her heated flesh and let his body fill her.

Blood, heated from their lovemaking, filled his mouth. He drank greedily from her wound as he came inside of her. She cried out again when he drew hard on her, and when she came again, he licked the wound closed and brought her to a third, then a fourth climax before he fell on top of her. He rolled to his back and pulled her with him, his cock still deep inside of her. Neither of them spoke, though he could feel her emotions now. Her thoughts went from sated bliss to embarrassment to anger in a few minutes. When she rolled off him, he let her go, knowing that she was going to tear him apart if he tried to hold her.

She stood up and staggered slightly, but before he could help her, she was pulling away. Grabbing up what was left of the shirt she'd had on, she glared at him. Alistair stood up and watched her.

"You could at least cover up." He looked down at his body. His cock, still wet from her, stirred. "I'm not going to do that with you again."

He didn't say anything, and was just glad that she hadn't claimed he'd forced her. When she went to the bedroom, he followed her. She turned and started to say something, but he held up his hand.

"This is my room where my clothes are. Unless you want me to be naked for this argument, I suggest you let me get dressed." She nodded, and he handed her a shirt and a pair of his boxers. She snatched them from him, and he had to turn his back or laugh. Christ, she was beautiful all tousled and pissed off like she was.

He pulled on a pair of his sweat pants, not bothering with either boxers or a shirt. If he had his way, they'd get into that bed she was currently sitting on and make love again. He watched her as she sat there.

"You could have said no." He shook his head. "I think that would have been the right thing to do. Or I guess I could have begged you less."

"You could have, but I'm certainly not going to complain." She stood up and put her hand on her side where she'd been shot. "Are you hurting? I'm sorry. I didn't think about that when we were making love."

"I didn't either, and for the record, we didn't make love. We had sex. Great sex, but there was no love involved." He couldn't argue with that. They didn't love each other, not yet at any rate. "I have to... I've never come before."

He stared at her for several seconds, not believing what she'd said. "You mean you've never enjoyed sex with your husband before? What a fool he was not to make sure you had your pleasure before him."

She laughed. "He said it was my fault. Of course, I never believed him. But still it was...frustrating not to.... Is it always like that with you?"

It was on the tip of his tongue to ask her if she'd like to find out, but only shook his head. He knew she was hurting, and not just from the wound. What they had done was too quick even for his kind. Alistair leaned forward in his chair and spoke to her softly.

"I never meant for that to happen. I just wanted you to trust me." She looked at him with a raised brow. "Okay, I did want that to happen, but not now, not when you don't trust me. I do want you to know that when I shifted I did only want to show you that I wasn't lying to you."

She nodded. "Are there more like you? I mean, I guess your brothers are, and your mom, but are there others? I read about wolves and panthers, too. Are they...?"

"Yes. The man who guards my brother's estate is a bear. Several wolves work for us in security as well as other jobs. I think there is a panther, too, but I can't remember if she's gone out on maternity leave or not yet."

She stood and looked at him, alarmed. "I'm not on the pill any more. I mean...I can't have your baby. I'm on the run too much to...I can't raise a baby like this. I just can't."

Alistair stood and walked to her. He took her into his arms and tried not to let it bother him that she was so stiff. He ran his fingers up and down her back as he tried to think how to tell her she wasn't going anywhere without pissing her off.

"I marked you, Allyson. As my mate, I marked you not only with my sperm but with my bite. I can't let you go, and I won't let him hurt you. Not ever, I swear to you." She pulled back and looked up at him. "I'm very possessive and you…please don't take this the wrong way, but you belong to me now, and I can't let you go."

She pulled away. Although it hurt, he let her. "I can't stay here, Alistair. If I do, when Lance comes here—and he will—I won't let him do to you what he's done to so many others. He's not a nice person, and he won't stop until he brings me home."

"He will have to learn to live with disappointment." She laughed. "I'm serious. You'll be safe here with us. No one will be able to come here without our knowledge. Haven't you read that we're the greatest trackers in the world?"

"Hum. I thought you said you were tiger, not wolf." It took him several seconds to realize she'd just teased him. And when he went after her she turned and stumbled into the bed. He reached up to the post closest to him and held it. It was either that or join her.

"You should know that I would like nothing better than to make love to you again. I would love to spread your thighs and drink from you. Having you come while I feast on you would make me so hard that when I entered you you'd feel it to your throat." He flared his nostrils. "I can smell you. The sweet perfume of your arousal is making my tiger want to taste you as well."

She didn't move when he let go of the post and moved up behind her. She was on her hands and knees, and he wanted more than anything to take her this way, press her into the mattress, and fill her with his cock as he bit her. Rolling her to her side, she moved to her back.

"Now would be a good time to tell me no." He reached down and slid his hand up the too large leg of his boxers she had on. "If you don't, I'm going to eat you until you scream."

Her legs opened, and he could smell all of her. As he pulled off the shorts, he asked her to take off the shirt. She pulled it up and over her head, then dropped it to the side of the bed onto the floor.

"Beautiful. So very beautiful, and all mine." Watching her face, he ran his fingers through her wet curls and coated them with her cream. Slowly, he took them to his mouth and sucked them clean. Her moan made him want more, made him want to do more for her.

He then lifted her ass up and buried his nose in her sweet heat. Licking her, then pressing his tongue deep into her, he moaned at her taste. She was so delicious that he knew that having her come in his mouth was going to be as close to paradise as he'd ever been. He suckled her hard nubbin, and her hips danced against his mouth.

Next, he curled his hands around her thighs and spread her nether lips open for him. She was so wet that he felt her juices as they ran down his chin and onto the bed. When her hand wrapped into his hair, he slid his fingers into her pussy and fucked her with his tongue and fingers until she cried out. Her release was just that; a flooding of her juices filled his mouth and body as he drank deeply from her. When she came again, crying out his name, he knew he had to be inside of her. Moving up her body, biting and tasting her as he went, he tore his pants off and fisted his cock. She looked up at him.

"I'm going to come in you, and when I do I want you to bite me. I want to feel your teeth draw blood. Drink from me." She nodded and reached for him.

He didn't just enter her but slammed into her. She was so tight around him he felt her sheath as she rippled around him. He sucked her breast. His canines dropped and he tasted blood. Moaning and fucking her as hard as he could, he moved to her shoulder and licked along the muscle there.

"Bite me. Christ, do it so I can fill you." Her mouth slid across his shoulder. When she licked him, her hot tongue tasting him, he felt his cock spilling into her. Pulling her to him and burying her face into him, he felt her sink her teeth into him. He roared out his release, and then took her throat.

She screamed, and he felt her come again and again. When she dropped her arms, he licked the wound closed and took her through another climax before his body couldn't move again. When he rolled over, he took her with him.

"You'll have to lick the wound, love. If you don't, it won't seal." Her tongue lapped across his shoulder and he felt his cock stir. He wasn't sure if he'd live through another climax.

"I guess there's nothing wrong with me when it comes to having a climax." Alistair laughed and lifted her chin to look at her. "That was amazing."

He reached for a blanket and pulled it over them after kissing her gently on the mouth. It occurred to him at that moment that he'd not kissed her. Lifting her chin up again he kissed her, gently and softly, before letting her lay back down.

"Now behave or I won't be able to move again. You've completely worn me out." She giggled, and he thought that he'd give anything in the world to hear her do that again. "When we wake up, I'll make you a proper dinner. Then, we'll come back up here and see if I can give you a better adjective than 'amazing' to say about the best sex I've ever had."

She giggled again and he held her until he was sure she was asleep. When he slipped out from under her he tucked her in and went to his office. He had to make some calls to get this thing with her ex-husband settled. The man was going to have to see that the better man won.

The first person he called was his brother, Keith. "I need you to run a check on a Lance Isaac. He's an attorney. And then a check on Allyson, his ex-wife." Keith asked him if this was about his mate, and he told him it was.

"Good. You know that I'm happy for you and all, but you do realize that it's like four in the morning, right?" Alistair looked at his watch and apologized. "No worries, but you owe me. And I want you to introduce me to her not as the 'geek' brother but as the professional computer programmer. I'm sick of being called the geek."

"Done. So long as you know that as soon as she meets you she's going to know you're a geek. Perhaps you should not carry a laptop with you everywhere you go and try to find a conversation that doesn't mention terabytes and band waves. Unless it's about an actual band, which I'm pretty sure you would know about, too."

"Yeah, yeah bite me, you asshole. Are you going to be up for the rest of the night?" He could hear the clicking of a keyboard as Keith started on the project. "I might have a question or two to ask you, and I wouldn't want to disturb you guys."

Alistair looked at the ceiling above him, knowing that she was in his bed sleeping. But as much as he wanted to join her there again, he knew that this was important, too. He told Keith he'd be up. After hanging up he called the chief of police and talked to him about the murders at the courthouse.

"I'm telling you this because you're my friend and I like to run with you. But first, did you and Brock come into the building after hours the other night? The reason I'm asking is because I could smell you in places you guys don't normally go." Clifton Slone was a werepanther and his close friend. "And if you did, I don't suppose you found your girl, did you?"

"Off the record?"

"Yes."

"Then we did. Why? What did you find out?"

"Nothing, but that she was hiding away in the sublevels and that there was blood there. Then I got yours and who I thought was Brock's scent." He paused. "Is she the one that saved you?"

"Yes. And she's my mate, too." There was a long silence this time that made him nervous. Before he could ask again what he'd found out his friend spoke.

"Her prints come up on another charge...not murder but robbery. But there's something hinky about it, just so you know. Her prints didn't come up until five days later. And you'll never guess who added them in."

"Lance Isaac."

"Yes."

"You said hinky. What do you mean exactly? Do you think he might have put them in on his own?"

"Yes. What do you know about her ex? Other than he's a shark of a lawyer? A fucking prick and a general dumbass if he thinks people don't know he's also a lousy piece of shit. Not to mention a Grade A asshole."

"Wife beater? Son of a bitch that's going to lose the best thing he ever had? I have a whole list of names if you want to know the truth. Are you thinking that they might not be true?"

Clift laughed. "Oh no, they're true, alright, and that man has a real hard-on to find his wife, I guess. When her prints hit, he called here about five seconds later, like he was watching for them."

Alistair decided to beef up his security both at home and around the family by calling in a few favors. He knew firms that could do it so that no one could enter his home.

"Something else...he says that she's still his wife. Looked it up just before you called, and she filed the papers and all, so you can add *fucking liar* to your list."

They talked for a few more minutes, slowly moving from Lance to running in the woods behind his house. Clift said that he needed to get out there, and Alistair told him he had an open invitation.

Alistair heard Allyson stirring around seven and went to the kitchen to start some breakfast. His cook wasn't due until eight, but he wanted to cook for her himself. When she came down she was wearing another of his shirts and a pair of his boxers. He thought about giving her clothes to her but decided he liked her better this way.

KATHI S. BARTON

CHAPTER 4

Lance waited for over an hour for the cop to call back, and when he didn't, he made arrangements to go to him. He had the family jet standing by readying a flight plan when his mother, Aida Smyth Isaac, walked in. She glared at him as he hung up the phone.

"We're in a money crisis and you're making arrangements to go flying across the States? If you think I'm going to stand by while you take another bimbo off to who cares where, you're sadly—"

"I found her. She's in Ohio. I'm going there now to bail her out of whatever mess she's gotten herself into and bring her home. She'll not leave me again before I can get this shit settled."

"She divorced you. How do you suppose you're going to get anything settled? Without a marriage certificate, a valid one, you're never going to make the insurance company pay off when she's dead. And I do hope you plan better with this one than you did the last bride. She lived a little too long, and now look what's happening. We're in deeper now than we were before. I'd like one of these women to pay off, not drain us dry, if you don't mind."

His mother had a way about her that made him want to blow her fucking brains out and piss on them for good measure. He sat back in his chair and actually contemplated it. Maybe when he finished with Allyson he'd take out a policy out on her. Just for the fun of it. But he did think about his second wife. She'd been a drain on their already low resources and when she died, thanks to his working knowledge of life support systems, he'd had to find another wife quickly and had ended up with Allyson and her mother.

His family was broke. Not just that they couldn't afford to take long vacations in Paris, but that the house in France had been sold off to pay the taxes on the house here in the States, as was any other property they had owned. This house and the jet were all they had left. And now that he was under review again for something at work, he wasn't drawing a pay check either. As much as he wanted to blame this on Allyson, he couldn't, not really. They were broke when he married the first time, and that wife had been killed.

He'd had nothing to do with her death. It just happened, and because it had happened in a building that had lax security systems in place, he'd sued. With the double insurance pay off and the settlement, he'd done very well. But the money hadn't lasted nearly as long as he thought it should have. It might have if he didn't had to have so much fun, but having fun to Lance was what it was all about.

Then he'd married the second time to Paula Cook. She was a cow, but a rich one. After about six months of marriage, he started giving her a little something extra in her tea. He had thought that cyanide would have worked faster, but it hadn't, and he'd increased the dosage several times over the ensuing months only to have it be for nothing. Then she had a stroke, and they'd run all sorts of tests and found that her liver was bad, and a great many other problems. Had he just waited, she would have died on her own, but they marked her down as suicide because she had to have known that she was dying, and he didn't get shit except a great many hospital bills that were still unpaid. Her rich fuck of a daddy wouldn't help either, because he never believed his daughter, his precious little girl, would do such a thing to herself. He had on his list of new wives to find that no daddies should be in the way. If there was, he'd take care of them before they were married.

"Are you listening to me?" He looked at his mother and stood up. No, he hadn't been, and he didn't want to now. He had other things to do, and if he stayed there with her a minute longer, he wasn't going to be responsible for what happened to her. Well, he would, but he wasn't going to take blame for it. He pulled his coat on and grabbed his cell phone.

"I'm going to go and get the little bitch and bring her back here. You want to be helpful, why don't you plan a nice little wedding for us for when I get back? Even if I have to drug the cunt, we'll be married. Then, when the time is right, she'll meet with an untimely death...or I should say *timely* death, like her predecessors did." He stopped at the doorway. "You might want to find another wifey for me, too. I have a feeling that we're going to need a tad more than this one is going to bring us, the way my job is going."

He was driving to the airstrip when his phone rang. He didn't recognize the number, but thinking it could be the police, he answered. He snarled at the woman on the other end when she launched into a tirade about how his hospital bills were about to be turned over to a collection agency, and that she'd give him a nice little discount if he paid right now, while she had him on the phone. He told her to fuck off and hung up.

The pilot eyed him when he ran up the stairs. He was sure that he was pissed about the last two checks that had bounced. *Well, fucktard, when you demand payment from a broke fuck like me, you should ask for cash.* He settled into his seat and waited for him to say something. If he did, Lance was going to come up out of his chair and kill the man; he was that close to the edge. The pilot moved to the front of the plane and announced that they were in line to be able to take off. It should be only a few more minutes.

Lance knew after sitting without moving for the better part of two hours that his pilot was doing this on purpose. He had no one to send up front to make him get going, and if he got up to do it himself, it would be a defeat. So Lance watched some of the movie that was playing and did a little pretend work on his phone, which mostly consisted of him playing a game. When the plane moved, he put it away and tried to appear as relaxed as possible. He would win this round if it killed him.

They landed in Ohio two hours later. He had no idea how long it should have taken, but he was so pissed by the time he got off the plane that one word from anyone would have had him in prison for murder. He went to the desk to ask if there was a car for him to rent.

After forty-five minutes of trying to get the woman to simply give him the car, that he was good for the money, he gave up and went to find a taxi. Apparently, his credit card company had closed his account. Fucking assholes. He hated everyone right now. When he cleared the checks from the death of Allyson he was going to shove it up all their asses and hope it hurt. Christ, his head hurt.

The ride cost him over twenty bucks. He wished now that he'd stayed home and that he'd never heard of Allyson Lacey. But for Christ's sake, he needed just one break, just one thing to go right, and hoped to hell that the police station had some good news. But, of course, the man he needed to speak to was gone for the day.

The only thing he could afford was the cheapest hotel he could find in the worst part of town. He called his mother and told her that he needed money. He had to wait for five full minutes for her to stop laughing before she asked him if he thought she could shit him some. This day was becoming a real fuck up, and his mother was being a real cunt.

"Sell something. I don't care what it is, but I need money. How the hell am I supposed to make my wife come back to me if I can't even get her back to the airport but on my fucking back? Right now, I don't even have enough money to buy a soda from the vending machine, much less eat." He waited for her to say something, and when she did, he wasn't sure she was going to be around much longer. He was most definitely going to shoot her when he returned.

"I'll sell something of yours. I'll take some of those suits you have in the closet wasting space. You have more than you can wear in a month. And where would you even wear them? You have no job." She went on to list other things of his she could sell. He finally hung up when she mentioned his cufflink collection. If she even thought of selling that, he'd walk back to Nevada and strangle her.

He heard from her over three hours later. She'd actually sold his cufflinks. "I'm sending you half of what I got for them. The other is going for my hair. I've not had it done in months and people are beginning to talk."

Lance was sure that his mother's lack of hairstyle was going around the circuit like a wave at a football game. When he asked her how much she'd gotten, she pretended not to have heard him. He was almost afraid to go to the local drugstore and find out. An hour later he was watching the clerk count out fourteen hundred dollars to him; far less than he'd paid for even one of his sets. No more threats, he was most assuredly going to murder her.

~~~

"He's behind in his taxes as well as his credit card bills and all his utilities. The only thing he's not behind on is his cell phone, but that's past due and about ready for another payment. If he doesn't pay, who knows? And also the insurance policy he has on you." Ally looked at Keith as he spoke.

"On me?" Ally said. "Why does he have a policy on me?" Keith looked at Alistair, so she knew something was wrong. "What is it? Please tell me. I don't want something to happen to you all since you have it in your head that I'm not leaving here. So spill it."

"Did you know that your ex-husband was married twice before?" Alistair asked. She nodded. "What did you know about them?"

Ally looked at Keith, then at Alistair. "He said that his first wife, Delia, was killed in a building where the security was lax and he sued them. His second wife...I don't remember her name...died of a heart attack. He said she was overweight and didn't take care of herself. Why?"

"His second wife was Paula Cook-Isaac. Her father, Marcus Cook, thinks that Lance was poisoning her." She sat back in the chair and tried to think why Alistair would even think this when he continued. "I know that you probably don't believe me, but it's true. Ryland just spoke to him about an hour ago, right after we talked to Keith."

She looked down at the papers that Keith had handed her when she'd first come in the office. She'd been embarrassed because Alistair was dressed in a suit and she was still wearing his boxers and a shirt that was miles too big for her.

At least she had a bra on now. She picked up the folder and looked at the papers inside of it again.

"You think that he's paying my policy so that when he gets me back he'll kill me in some horrific way and collect. Makes sense, I suppose, but it won't work if we're not married, will it? I mean, why would anyone believe that he's paying an insurance company on a policy on me when we're not even married?"

"He can take out an insurance policy on whomever he wants. So long as he has nothing to do with the death and he pays the premiums, he can collect. Marrying you or being married to you makes little difference, so long as he has all the information that they require. But like I said, he has to make all the payments." She looked at Alistair, suddenly very afraid. "Getting you back to him? I would imagine that he'd have control when you died rather than it happening later."

"He told me when he first hit me the first time that he was under a lot of stress. He said he had a great many bills that his wife had acquired when she'd fallen ill. Then, there was the problem he was having at work." She looked at Keith this time. "I don't suppose you know what that was about, do you?"

Alistair cleared his throat, and she looked at him. "He hit his secretary this time. Before her there were five more that he supposedly hurt. But they dropped the charges after the thing went public. Then, after he was brought before the board on ethics charges, he was told there was some missing money from the firm where he works, as well. They have since suspended his license to practice law in Nevada."

"Danielle Smart, right?" He nodded. "He told me that she tried to tell his boss that he'd made advances toward her. Although I have no idea why he'd think anyone would want to sleep with him. He's selfish in bed and doesn't care about his partner."

Ally flushed when she realized what she'd said. Keith started to laugh but turned it into a cough when Alistair looked at him. She felt sorry for him and stood up to pace.

"I'm not going to tell you again that you should just let me go away. When he gets here, you have to know that he has a temper and that he's going to be mad. I'd rather not get you hurt again."

"You didn't in the first place. A man bent on killing a circuit court judge did, and he didn't hurt me thanks to you." She nodded at him but was not really paying any attention. She was trying to think about something that Lance had said to her a long while back.

"He told me once that when the chips were down he could always depend on his backup plan. What do you suppose he meant by that?" She looked at them both. "You think he has money stashed somewhere?"

"Doubtful. But he might. I'll keep looking." Keith stood up to leave and then looked at his brother. "You owe me."

Alistair stared at him for a long moment, and she thought there was something going on that he wasn't happy about. When he nodded, Keith put his laptop down and pulled her to him. She was so startled that she wrapped her arms around him to keep from falling. He held her without saying anything. Then he reached down and kissed her forehead. Smiling, he picked up his things and left without a word. She looked at Alistair.

"You remember me telling you that I'm a tad possessive?" She nodded. "I told Keith that if he found anything on Lance that was worthy that I'd let him hug you. The kiss was his idea."

"I don't understand. Why did you think that hugging me would be worth anything to him? I mean, I'm not really anything special, just a woman on the run from her ex-husband. Why would you give him that as a gift?"

"Because he knew it would bother me for him to touch you. Not just touch you, but to hold you. Cats, especially werecats, are very territorial and extremely possessive. Not with their things, such as cars, homes, or anything like that, but with mates…with a mate all bets are off. That's why we need to mate and bond so quickly. The need to…I guess dominate the female so that she'll know who is the boss is there, but with another male it's like we're ape-shit possessive. Under other circumstances, I would kill him."

"So you gave me to him to hug." He stood up and came to her. She had no idea why she was so hurt. When he pulled her into his arms, she tried to pull back, but he was stronger. For that reason alone, she was hurt more.

"I didn't mean to hurt you. If you…." He took a deep breath. "I'm sorry. If you knew how it made him feel to have permission to hug you, then you'd understand why I did it. But I should have explained to you first. I should have told you what an honor you were giving him by letting him hold you in his arms."

"An honor?" He nodded. "I don't think I understand this thing. I mean, I go for years and years with no desire to have sex with anyone, and boom, you come along and the first time we're together we're going at it like rabbits. I'm not that person."

She looked at him when he laughed. "I'm sorry. But rabbits? Okay, I understand what you mean, though. The first time I caught your scent I wanted you. I'm not really sure why it works that way, unless it's some internal code to mark our family and compel us to multiply, but it's there. You felt it, too."

"The first time I saw you, all I could think about was that man was going to kill you and then me. I remember thinking that I'd rather go out of this world a hero and not the victim of spousal abuse." She turned away from him. "This is going so fast, Alistair. I'm so afraid."

"I know, baby. And I promise you that I'll protect you… all of us will. Ryland is working on things now to keep you safe so we can go out. And Bronwyn is going to go with you to buy some clothes. She's scary when it comes to what she can do."

Bronwyn scared her, too. The woman had only spoken to her once, and Ally felt as if she was being grilled for some sort of clearance to a big government facility. But she also had a feeling she was being sized up for something. Ally looked at Alistair.

"I have a favor to ask. It's not a big one, but would you mind not calling me Allyson? Lance did that, and I always think of him when you do it. Most of my friends and my mom called me Ally. Just Ally." He nodded. "And we need some ground rules here. I know that you have this tiger thing going on, but I don't. I'm not…Christ, I never thought I'd say this, but I can't do sex like you do all the time."

"You're sore." She nodded and flushed so deeply that she felt the heat over her entire body. "I can understand that. You need to get used to me wanting you all the time anywhere I can get you naked. I'll only make love to you three times a day and not ten. All right?"

She looked at him with her mouth open, and when he pushed it closed, she knew he'd been kidding. Or at least she thought he was. She backed up when he reached for her. His chuckle made her pinch his arm.

"I was kidding you. And I'm sorry. I should have realized that with a selfish partner like Lance, you'd be sore when you had a real man between your legs." He laughed when she pinched him again. "Christ, you're going to be fun to live with for the rest of our lives."

Bronwyn came by to get her an hour later. By then she'd been given strict instructions to stick with her like glue four times, and had been lectured twice on the money being theirs and not his any longer. He'd given her a list of things to purchase, and she wasn't to come back until she had all of it. When she got into the large SUV with Bronwyn, she glared at the list. Bronwyn took it out of her hand and read it over.

"He actually told you to buy three dozen pairs of sexy underwear?" She nodded. "Does he think you're a simpleton?"

"No. He said he wants to tear them off me, and if I have enough of them, we could go for a couple of days without me being without under things." She turned away when Bronwyn laughed. "I don't know why I agreed to this. I should be making plans to get away from here, not going on a shopping spree like I have nothing at all going on in my life."

"You leave and I'll kick your ass." Ally looked at her and knew she was telling the truth. "I think we should forget about his list and have fun. Oh, I hope you don't mind, but Sandra is going to meet us there. She said she wanted to get to know you better. I think she just wants to find out if Alistair is treating you right."

"He is. I mean, he's better than…." She frowned. "I started to say he was treating me better than my last lover, but that's not true. Alistair is nothing like I've ever seen before, much less been with. He's kind and giving. I've never met anyone like him before."

"They're all like that." Bronwyn drove for a little while before she spoke again. "Keith told me that you let him hug you. You made him feel really special for doing that."

"I had no idea that it was such a big deal. I still don't understand it, really. I know that Alistair said that it's a mate thing, but I have been hugged by men before. It's never been a big deal."

"It is now. Trust me. And just while we're talking about them, have you been told that Ryland is the leader of the family? And as his mate, I'm the she-leader. I don't understand why there's a need for a pecking order, but there is."

"Alistair told me. He said that before his dad died he was leader." Bronwyn nodded. "Can I ask you something?"

"Sure. And so you know, what you ask me will be answered honestly and directly. If you really don't want the answer, I suggest that you rethink the question."

Ally nodded. "What are you?" Ally watched her face as Bronwyn thought about it. She thought she might be pissy about it, but she didn't appear to be. When she smiled at her, Ally smiled back.

"How much do you know about magic?" Ally shrugged. "Me either, but I can do a shit-ton of crap about it. Move things, bend metal. I can also play with your mind. I can make you think things I want you to, see whatever it is I need you to see, and do things that you wouldn't normally ever do on your own. I can shift into any animal I want, but there are drawbacks. If I've never seen the animal shift, I might get it a little wrong. And I can heal you."

"Heal me? You mean if I get a cut or something?" Bronwyn nodded then shook her head. "You mean that you can bring-me-back-from-the-dead kind of heal me?"

"Not that far, but when you're close I can. It takes a great deal out of me, but I can do it." Bronwyn parked the car and asked her for her hand; she gave it to her without hesitation. "I can tell that you're terrified of your relationship with Alistair. You're also afraid that when Lance comes here, he'll harm one or more of us. May I touch your head?"

Ally was afraid, but nodded. When she touched her forehead, Ally felt the connection immediately and profoundly. Then when the images started to roll forward, she watched as Lance moved through the parking lot of some hotel, she saw his mom talking to him on the phone, telling him that he needed to get her and to get his ass back home. She saw Alistair sitting at his desk, staring at the computer, and she saw Mrs. Golden approach them in a shop that sold bath soaps. When she let her go, Ally felt dizzy, and she could only stare at Bronwyn.

"Are those real?" Bronwyn nodded. "He's here then, isn't he? Lance is in this state looking for me right now?"

"Yes. He arrived yesterday afternoon." Ally waited for her to tell her that things were going to be taken care of, but she didn't say anything like that. All she said was he would be really stupid if he tried anything while they were shopping.

She got out of the car with her and they moved into the mall. She was almost afraid to go in because she was afraid he'd be there.

Bronwyn put her arm around her and whispered, "If he were here, I'd tell you, but he's not. Let him go for now. There's not a fucking thing he can do to you here. Not while any of us are with you. You're as safe as you'll ever be, trust me."

Ally looked at her. "I'm trying to trust, but it's a little overwhelming. What if he—?"

"You could 'what if' until hell freezes over, but it won't mean shit when it comes down to it. He's not here. You have an endless credit card and more shops in this mall than any other in the world. We're going to have fun."

CHAPTER 5

Ryland watched Alistair. He would stare off into space for a few minutes, then back at him like he had no idea what they'd been talking about. The first few minutes of teasing him had been fun, but now he was just worried. When he looked at him again, Ryland told him what he was doing.

"You miss her." Alistair nodded. "It's not easy when you're first together. It's like you can't get enough of each other. And the need to touch is overwhelming."

"Christ, it's like if I'm not touching her, I'm going to go crazy. And then touching leads to wanting her. Then sex. She'd never come before me." Ryland had to bite the inside of his mouth when Alistair turned as red as a beet. "I didn't mean to say that. But I can't help but feel like a million bucks when I think of it."

He didn't say anything. Not that he was sure what he would say because he knew what it was like to have a mate that loved sex as much as he did. Ryland was trying to think of something clever and witty to say when Alistair's phone rang. Alistair picked it up and barely said his name when he looked at him with a look of fear. Something had happened. Ryland reached for his mate, but she was blocking him. He was ready to go find her when Alistair spoke.

"We'll be right there." His voice was calm, but Ryland could feel his terror. "Yes, you're right. Yes, Ryland is right here with me. I'll…yes, I'll bring him, too." When he hung up, Ryland was ready to strangle him.

"There's been a shooting at the mall," Alistair said. "Bronwyn said that they were shopping and someone came in with a gun and started mowing people down. Mom and Ally are fine, as is Bronwyn." Ryland didn't respond, knowing that there was more. "He just opened fire on the store that they were in, and Bronwyn said that he was looking for Ally. He was looking to kill my Ally."

Ryland was afraid, too. This had gone beyond a simple ex-husband trying to get his wife to come back to him to outright murder. He guided his brother out to his car and even buckled him in. As they drove to the mall, he reached out to Bronwyn.

"We're all fine. I swear to you we're all fine." He felt his body relax just hearing her voice. *"He killed nine people, including a small child. He wanted Ally, but he couldn't find her. I couldn't protect them all."*

"I know, love. You protected what you could, I have no doubt. What do you know about him? Anything? Is he dead?"

"Yes, dead. I didn't mean to kill him, but he just wouldn't stop coming. It was as if he was on something or someone was controlling him." He didn't want to believe it, but she'd know more than anyone. *"Ryland, he was sent here to find her by someone other than Lance. He wasn't in his mind at all."*

"You mean that there's someone else trying to kill her?" She told him *yes,* and Ryland looked over at his brother. *"Does she know? Does Ally know?"*

"No. She said that she'd never seen him before, but she's looking like she might have remembered something about

him. I was going to look, but I don't want to hurt her. She's pretty fragile right now. And she needs Alistair."

"He needs her, too. He's sort of in a zombie-like state. Has been since you called him, and way before that, I think. We're nearly to the parking lot now." He looked around and wondered how he was supposed to find them. *"Honey, I don't know how we're going to get to you. There's a lot of news vans here already."*

"Go to the food court entrance. There'll be a mall cop standing there. His badge says his name is...." She laughed. *"His name is Lance. He's a tall guy and he'll show you how to get here if you tell him your name."*

When he turned off the car Alistair looked at him. He looked like he was coming back to himself now, and Ryland waited for him to say something. He looked up to make sure that the mall cop wasn't waiting on them before looking at his brother again.

"You've spoken to Bronwyn?" Ryland nodded. "She said that Ally was fine, but all I could think about was that I hadn't been there to protect her when I told her I would."

"You did protect her. If you had been with her instead of Bronwyn, you'd both be dead. You protected her." Alistair nodded.

"He was gunning for her, wasn't he? The man that shot at them, he was coming for Ally like she told me on the phone?" Ryland told him that was what Bronwyn had said. "Is it anything to do with her ex?"

"No, or it doesn't appear so. Bronwyn said Ally is pretty shook up. You ready to go and hold her?" Alistair nodded but didn't move. "Alistair, it's going to be all right. We're going to protect her."

"I know that, but what if the next time no one is there to protect her? Whoever this is means to have her dead, not just back like her ex does. How can I keep her safe from things I don't know?" Ryland didn't know how to answer that, so he didn't. "I don't want to lose her, Ryland. I don't want to sound like a sap, but I already love her and I can't lose her."

He got out before Ryland could say anything. He knew how his brother felt. Having a mate, someone to love him no matter what, was the best thing that had ever happened to him. He followed his brother in just as the mall cop was coming toward them. He nodded when Ryland told him his name and started back the way he'd come. When he saw Bronwyn with Ally and his mom, he nearly wept with relief. Alistair took off running and grabbed Ally up as soon as she leapt into his arms. Ryland wanted to do the same to his mate, but she was dealing with a newsman who was trying to get her to tell him what had happened. He stood by to watch the show.

"You put that fucking thing in my face again, I will shove it so far up your ass that you're going to need to learn to shit from your nostrils. I said I do not want to speak to you or your mother fucking viewers. You want to interview somebody, go over and ask that woman whose little boy was gunned down by that fucking cocksucker over there and see how entertaining she can be." The guy pulled his microphone back from Bronwyn like she really was going to hurt him with it. Ryland was pretty sure she would, too.

"You were there. We just want to—" She slugged him. Hard and in the nose. As soon as blood started to erupt from his face, she asked the cameraman if he was getting this. When he backed away from her, she smiled.

"You use any of this footage on your program and I will hunt you down and shove that camera so far down your throat that they won't be able to bury you without it. Got it?" The man nodded, opened his camera, and handed her the little card.

"You keep it," the cameraman said." "We'd have to bleep every word you said anyway, and unlike him, I can see that you're serious that you don't want to be interviewed." He moved away from her without another word.

Bronwyn turned to Ryland and wrapped her arms around him. He laughed when she told him she had been so scared. When she pulled back and frowned, he kissed her on the nose.

"You might have been scared, but that man over there has you beat. I'm reasonably sure that if another woman tells him she doesn't want to be interviewed, he'll walk away."

She smiled at him and moved back when his mom came toward them. Alistair was still holding onto Ally, and he kept an eye on them both. This wasn't a good place to fall apart. When Bronwyn looked around, he asked her if they should be worried about anyone there.

"No. I just…." She looked around again. "There's something off here. Don't you think? Look around and tell me what you see."

He held her to him and looked around. There were several news crews talking into mikes or interviewing people. He saw the cameramen standing very still as they filmed the anchors. Mall security was milling about with the police, and there were several hundred shoppers staring on as if they were waiting for someone to open fire again. Then he looked into the store.

The front window was filled with half-dressed mannequins as well as a large bathtub filled with what appeared to be silver balloons. Ryland thought it was supposed to be bubbles and thought that they'd done a good job of it. Towels hung over the edge and draped to the floor, and a dark pink and red shower curtain hung behind the scene so that it looked like a bathroom. He looked at the doorway into the shop, then back at the scene.

"How did he see you?" Bronwyn nodded. "Where were you in the shop when the shots started firing?"

"In the back. We were trying to talk Ally into a lovely bra-and-panty set when I felt him coming toward us. Before I could step in front of your mom and Ally, the cashier was killed."

"He knew Ally was in the shop." She nodded again, and he felt a shiver run up his spine. "Did you get anything from him prior to him shooting the place up?"

"Only that he had a clear picture which one she was and that he was to kill her at all costs. He was excited to be able to take out so many with her, as well." She turned in his arms, and he held her. "There are four people in the crowd with cell phones that are recording this. Two more behind us that are talking about how they're going to be famous at school in the morning when word gets out they were here. There is a woman in the shop still that won't come out because she wet herself, and the woman with her is trying her best not to tell the girl she'd done the same thing. But there is no one here that has a clue what happened or why other than us."

Ryland nodded to Alistair when he caught his eye. It was time to move them out before whoever ordered this showed up to finish the job. He was just turning to leave with them all when Bronwyn touched his arm. He stilled and watched her as she spoke to Ally.

"They're going to say you're dead." Ally started to shake her head. "It'll come out later that you're not, but for now, they're going to assume you're among the dead. It will buy us some time in trying to figure this out."

Ally looked at the man that had been covered up, then back at them. "You'll tell me what you know. I know you said you can do a shit ton of stuff, so I'm guessing you know what is really going on here, right?"

"Yes. He wasn't sent by your ex. According to what I've found out and what Keith has, I would assume that you're worth more to your ex alive than dead right now."

"If he tries to cash in on another insurance scam with a dead wife, somebody might notice something. That's why he wants me to go back, so he can marry me again and make a claim when I'm dead." Ryland looked at Alistair, who looked as shocked as he felt. "I'm not stupid, and I can look things up. If he makes another claim, especially on a divorced wife, someone might look deeper into what he's done before. And from what you told me this morning, he can't afford that."

"I didn't say you were stupid, and believe me, if I thought so I would tell you." Bronwyn took a deep breath. "Let's get out of here now before some asshole comes along and shoots us for simply being here."

~~~

Ally crossed her arms over her chest and glared at the men and woman staring at her. She was as pissed as she'd ever been. She moved back when Alistair stood up.

"I'm not happy with you, either." He sat back down. "And just so you know, right now you can all bite my ass. I'm not going to put any of you in danger. I'm leaving."

"So you said. Four times now." Jules stood up. "I'm going home. I've got three pieces I have to finish before next week, and arguing with a woman bent on getting herself killed isn't getting them done. And just so you know, I would die for you right now. You're his mate, no matter if you're here or not; and you dying will kill him."

"What do you mean?" Jules turned back to her and smiled, but not a smile she thought of as warm and friendly. She took a step back. He stepped toward her.

"Like him, I won't ever harm you, but that doesn't mean that I'll stand in front of you to get shot while you run in the opposite direction. He will die if you leave him, because he would go and hunt down your ex just to keep you with him. And he'd do it alone, without telling us, because he knows, like you, that your ex-husband will hurt us. Like we give a shit where a mate is concerned. We protect what is ours. Period."

"Lance will hurt him." Jules cocked a brow at her. "Okay, he'll try to hurt him. What does that have to do with me leaving now? Lance doesn't know about any of you."

Keith stood up and handed her a large phone-like object. Jules took it from her and turned it on before giving it to her again. There they all were standing in front of the store after the shooting. She looked up at him, not understanding why he had this.

"It's on all the social networks. Some kid must have recorded it and posted it. I can take it down, but it's gone viral and been shared by nearly ten million people. I'll never get them all taken down before Isaac might see it." Keith nodded to the device she had in her hands as he continued. "I found that just simply by putting in mall shooting. There are nearly a dozen more making the rounds."

She sat down. She looked at Bronwyn when she cleared her throat. The woman was going to tell her something she didn't want to hear, so she stood up again and started for the kitchen. She was pulling out flour and sugar when she heard someone enter.

"I'm going to bake something. Do you have any preferences? I have to bake something before I explode." She heard a small laugh and looked over at Alistair. "You think this is so fucking funny? That man shot all those people because he was looking for me. For me."

"And you want to bake." She didn't even answer as she opened the refrigerator and began to pull out eggs and milk. The cook, a very nice man by the name of Jed Richards who looked like a giant of a bear himself, only pointed to where things were when she asked him.

"You're frightening our cook." Jed snorted, then looked at Alistair when she did. "You are. He's afraid you'll mess up his lovely kitchen. Isn't that right, Jed?"

"Sir, I've served you for ten years, and in all that time I would scream at you for messing in my kitchen, that's true. You never put things away the way I want them, and you don't tell me when I've run out. But in all this time, never has a woman come in here demanding where I put my measuring spoons." Jed grinned at her as he handed down a large bowl from the cabinet over her head. "She can cook all she wants and leave me the mess to pick up. I don't ever, never ever, fuck with a mate that's as pissed as she is."

Ally laughed. She couldn't help it. Jed did look to be a little scared. He winked at her, and she asked him what he was, then flushed hotly when he laughed at her.

"I'm so sorry. That was rude and very…it was rude. I've never met a tiger before this and assumed since you said something about…." She put down the bowl with eggs in it and stepped from the counter. "I'm sorry. I had no right to come into your kitchen and act like this."

Alistair started to say something but Jed cut him off. He looked at Alistair, who nodded before turning back to her and smiling.

Jed handed her the bowl of eggs and a whisk. "I'm a tiger, like you, but I've been injured. My cat has been, anyway. He…well, he's a bit on the scared side now and hasn't been out to play in some time. He is afraid, you see."

"Afraid? I don't understand. Aren't you…you're a weretiger, right?" Jed nodded. "Then why is he afraid, and you aren't? And you aren't, are you?"

They both looked at Alistair when he cleared his throat. "While we reside in one body, we're as different as two separate people. He has his likes and dislikes, as his cat does. When his cat was injured, then…well, Jed can't shift."

She looked at them both, trying to figure out if they were kidding her. Her books had never said anything about them being two people, or in this case, a person and a cat. She started mixing the ingredients together while she thought about it. She heard the door open and close behind her but paid little attention. When she turned from putting the first pan of cookies into the oven, she was startled to see the entire family in there with her.

"I bake when I'm nervous." She started to clean up, and then decided that she needed more and pulled out some other things from the pantry and cabinets. "I like to make bread when I have a serious problem to work out. I've not had the…it's hard to bake when you're on the run."

Bronwyn snorted. "It's hard to bake when you're as big as a house, too. But I can sample anything you put before me. I love cookies and bread."

She put the milk on to cook and looked at them all, including Jed. "I don't know what to do. I mean, I know what I should do, but not what to do. Bronwyn told me that he's here in this area. He has to be looking for me here, so I'm assuming that the prints came back."

Alistair nodded before he answered her. "I spoke with a friend of mine, and he said he already spoke to your ex. He said the man claimed you were confused and that he should hold you until he got here. He also mentioned the robbery."

"Robbery? I don't know anything about…Lance did it?" He nodded at her. "When did this happen? I'm assuming that I should expect to be arrested soon?"

"No. Clift said that there was something wrong with the way they were added, and he's looking into that as well. You're safe here. And Isaac is in the area, but he doesn't seem to be having any kind of luck finding you. The police are…let's just say that he won't find too many people there that'll help him, if any at all." Alistair stood up and pulled on an oven mitt when the timer went off. Jed put out three cooling racks while she put in two more trays.

"So the police department is lying to a lawyer. That will get them into trouble, won't it?" Ryland grinned as he stuffed a hot chocolate chip cookie into his mouth. "You're going to burn yourself, you moron."

She took out a gallon of milk and handed it to him, then smacked him on the head when he started drinking from the jug. He got up to get glasses while she started to knead the bread. Jed sprinkled flour on the surface whenever she paused.

"Nah, we're not lying because none of them know for sure that you're here. Besides, as of two days ago, Isaac doesn't have a job, so he's not a lawyer. The police department will say that they're looking for you, or that they have some hits, but nothing solid. The only person who actually knows where you are, who has seen you here, is us. And we're not going to say anything to him." Ryland ate two more cookies as he spoke around them. "You know, these are amazing. And you didn't use a recipe or anything."

"I know how to bake. What do you mean no one knows but you guys? Are you saying that the cops know but they're going to tell him that since they've never seen me, it can't be proven? That's the stupidest thing I've ever heard." She looked at Jed when he laughed. "What do you think?"

"I think that if he is stupid enough to try and take you from anyone here, it's likely that he is stupid enough to believe that they've no idea where you are." He nudged her arm. "Knead and I'll make a dinner around this bread for you."

She looked around the room and settled her gaze on Bronwyn. "What is it you need to tell me? I'm assuming it has something to do with the mall shooting."

"Lance didn't send that man." Her world narrowed to a pinpoint and she felt arms around her. Then she was sitting in a chair with her head between her knees. It took her several minutes to realize that they were shouting at each other before she lifted her head. Putting two fingers into her mouth, she whistled. It froze everyone in place.

CHAPTER 6

Sandra was impressed. For a girl who said she wasn't much in the way of fighting back, she sure had these people thinking otherwise. When she ordered them to sit, all of them sat down, including Bronwyn and Ryland, without a single hesitation. Jed nearly did as well before she told him to help her with the flour.

"Now. We're going to do this calmly and without our loud voices. If you want to use them, you'll go outside and do it. You're terrifying me." She started to knead the bread again, and Sandra almost felt sorry for it. "Okay. Explain to me what you mean, Bronwyn."

Ally glared at Alistair when he opened his mouth, but when he closed it with an audible snap, Sandra had to cover her mouth with her hand. Yes, this girl would do well in this streak. Sandra thought maybe it might be fun to bait her, but decided that she'd do it later. Right now, there was just too much going on.

"Remember what I said about being able to do all sorts of stuff?" Ally nodded at Bronwyn. "Well, one of them, as you know, is reading minds. And I could feel the idiot coming toward the shop as we were coming out of the dressing room.

But he was a good deal closer to us than I thought, and I had no time to hide you, much less save everyone in the mall."

"Well, of course, you couldn't save everyone in the mall. How silly of you to think that you're that strong. And even if you had, how would you have been able to save your mother-in-law after draining yourself so much?" Ally looked at her. "She would have been too zapped to help us, wouldn't she?"

"Yes. It takes a great deal out of her when she uses her stuff. I'm sure that, had she more time to find and get rid of the man, she might have been too weak to save herself and my grandbaby." Sandra looked at Bronwyn. "You know what I'm telling her is the truth."

"Okay, then, you knew the man was coming, did your thing, and saved our butts. Then what? You read his mind and knew that someone else was sending him to kill me?" Ally looked at Jed and smiled. "I can't remember when I started doing this, do you?"

"It's kneaded enough, my dear." Sandra had a feeling the bread was perfect no matter what as she watched Jed prepare a bowl for it. "I'll just set this aside while we deal with the rest of these cookies."

There was a great deal more batter left, and as Jed scooped up the dough and dropped it on the sheet, Ally started to pace. Sandra watched her son. She knew that he loved the girl…it was written all over his face…but he also was afraid for her. Bronwyn started speaking as Ally pulled some other ingredients from the cabinets.

"I wasn't really sure what I was looking for, but I do know that your ex wasn't in his mind. So I dug a little deeper. I suppose that your ex could have sent him, but a female talked to him and told him where you were. She said that you'd either be in that particular shop or you'd be in the food court. Either way, he was excited to be getting to do this for her."

"I guess we should be lucky that he found me in the shop. There had to be considerably less people there." Ally was putting together something else in another large bowl while Jed finished the cookies off. It looked like ten or so dozen of them lay on several cooling racks on the counter.

Ryland got up to get more glasses as Bronwyn filled the plate again. If Ally kept this baking thing up she'd have enough food for the entire family to take home. She got up to find some old tins she knew that Alistair kept for her. She was just filling them with cookies when Ryland spoke.

"Do you know of any females that might want you dead? Or maybe someone that your ex might know that would help him? A friend or lover?" Ally shook her head as she poured sugar into the bowl.

"No. He didn't have many friends. People he worked with didn't care much for him, and I lost all of mine just after we were married. He had…I wasn't allowed to go out with them anymore without him, too." She looked up, pausing in the middle of mixing together the dry ingredients that Sandra just figured out was going to be pie crust. "Do you think it could have been his mom? I mean, she's as mean as a…she and I never seemed to get along, and the one time I went to her after I'd been returned home to see if she'd help me, she…."

Sandra felt the tension surrounding the girl and then noticed that even Jed took a step back. Alistair cleared his throat twice before he spoke, and even then his voice was hoarse and deep.

"What did she do?" Ally put the bowl onto the countertop and reached for the glass of ice water that Jed handed her.

"Ally, what did she do to you that made you not go back to her for help again?"

"She...she hit me. Not with her fists like Lance did, but with the mug she had in her hand. She told me that I should be grateful that she'd not come after me, because I wouldn't just need a long sleeved shirt like I needed to hide what her son had done. She'd...she said that she'd kill me if I ever tried to put her son into a position again where he had to explain what had happened to me. I knew then that I had to get away." She gently mixed the iced water with the dry things, making the dough soft and flaky. "She then told her son that I'd insulted him, and he said he'd take care of me when he got home. I ended up in the hospital then, and got out with the help of a nice judge."

"The one that had helped you with your divorce as well, correct?" Sandra looked at Keith when he spoke. "I helped find out all I could about you when you first got here. That was part of what I found. I'm sorry."

Sandra waited for a reaction from the girl—fireworks, anger, something—but all she did was shrug. Something was so...laid back about her that Sandra decided once she was able to let it go, she'd be hell on wheels.

The bread was punched down twice before the conversation was completed, and a loaf of it eaten as a snack when it came out of the oven while Jed cleaned up the kitchen. Most of the talk centered on family and antics of her son's childhood, but Sandra watched Alistair and Ally. She had never seen a couple bond so quickly and so completely before. And when he touched his mate, she could almost see the sparks flying.

"Dinner will be in one hour. I'm making fried chicken, mashed potatoes, white gravy, and green beans. The apple pie, my favorite, will not be shared." Jed grinned as he continued. "You've all eaten enough sweets for one day, and I shall sacrifice myself by eating the pie alone. In my room. With vanilla bean ice cream. And a cup of Londonderry tea."

They adjourned to the living room. Of course, no one believed Jed for a moment. Besides, Sandra was pretty sure that Bronwyn would murder him if he tried. This conversation was much different than the one in the kitchen. And Sandra was profoundly glad that things were going to start moving now.

~~~

Alistair watched his family with his mate. They were accepting and loving to her, and he was proud. He loved his family dearly, but if they had treated her with anything but respect, he would have no problem calling them out. He turned to Ryland when he said his name.

"Where were you, buddy? I was asking you if you heard anything back from your friend in Nevada." It took Alistair a few seconds to catch up. "The guy you said worked with Isaac?"

"Yeah. I heard from him last night by email. He said he'd call me tonight, but he said about the same things we already knew. His house is mortgaged to the max, and he is behind on everything. His car was repossessed about a month ago, and he's been telling people it was a mistake. And now he's reportedly telling everyone that he had gotten bored with having such a nice car and has decided to use a service." Alistair laughed. "He's into his service for nearly ten grand right now, so I doubt he'll be getting more rides from them."

"How did this happen?" Alistair looked at Ally when she asked. "I mean, they have several homes that are loaded with so many antiques that it boggles the mind. There used to be gardeners and maids, a cook, and someone on staff to watch the gates. When did all this go to shit?"

Neal cleared his throat. "I looked at the records. He's been overspending for nearly all his adult life. Both he and his mother have. Just before you left him this last time he took out another mortgage on his home. By the way, he forged your name to the loan, and until you divorced him, you were just as responsible for the debt as him. Your judge friend did an amazing job on your decree. He took your name off of everything and made sure that any money that was owed to creditors was only in your ex-husbands name."

"Judson Parrish…he was the judge that helped me. He said that he could make it so that I didn't actually need Lance's signature on the paperwork because of the abuse. He said that he'd fixed it so that anyone who saw me would know that he was a terrible prick and I deserved this." Ally flushed. "I'm sorry. You all must think I'm such a fool for marrying him in the first place."

"Did you love him?" They all looked at Jules, who had a plate of cookies in front of him. "I mean, at first, did you love him at all?"

"Yes. Well, at least I thought I did. My mother, you see, said that he would be good for me. He'd bring me out of my shell." Bronwyn snorted, and Ally laughed. "Yeah, I agree. He brought me out of my shell and right into intensive care."

"You do realize that when he figures out where you are that he's going to come here, right? So I'd like to make a few suggestions. I think—"

Cutting Bronwyn off, Alistair watched Ally stand. "I don't think you guys understand what kind of person he is. He's not going to just let this go. I've been thinking that if he comes here I should deal with him on my own."

"Are you fucking nuts?" Keith flushed. "Sorry. But well, no offense, but he's only a human. And we're…well, we're not. One of us could take him down and be done with it."

"I was going to say that you should learn to shoot." Bronwyn glared at Keith. "And taking him down, as you put it, would only solve part of the problem. There's still the person from the mall. She needs to learn to defend herself against pricks like that. She may not be able to stop bullets, but she can shoot back."

"I know how to shoot." Bronwyn raised a brow at her. "I'm pretty good, too. I've never killed anything, but I can hit a target."

"I don't think she's just talking about shooting a gun. I'm pretty sure she means defending yourself period. Like in hand-to-hand combat and any other thing that she can teach you." Alistair looked at Bronwyn, who nodded as he continued. "She can show you. I don't know if anyone has told you or not, but Bronwyn is one badass bitch."

"I am, too." Bronwyn laughed. "I can help you with this. Before I met Ryland and he forced me to like him, I was pretty good at taking on the bad guy and winning."

Alistair knew that they needed to get these two women together. Having Ally in shape to defend herself would help her with her confidence, too. Not that she was unsure of herself much, but he had seen her in the kitchen and she was terrified. He leaned back on the couch and listened to them talk. His phone vibrated in his pocket, and he pulled it out. The room grew quiet when he put up his hand.

"Hello?" There was a brief pause, but Alistair could hear the cars going by and someone mumbling in the background. He said *hello* again.

"Where is my wife?" Alistair took a notepad from the drawer on the coffee table and began writing. He handed it to Ryland as Isaac asked again.

"I don't know who you're talking about. Last I read somewhere you're divorced. So, are you married again?" The man started cursing and Alistair laughed at him. "You should really try to tone that down a bit there, big guy. People will get the impression that you're not a nice man."

Keith moved his fingers, plugged something into his phone, and started clicking on the computer he'd set up next to them. His brother was very good at his job.

"I don't know where you heard that at, but Allyson is my wife till death do us part. If she's there I want you to put her on the phone right fucking now. Tell her I've had enough of her bullshit." A car's horn beeped, and Alistair knew he was on a busy road. "I'm not fucking around here. I want her to get on this phone now."

"You think I'm just going to hand her the phone after that? Nah, don't think so. You could come here and see if she wants to talk to you. But I wouldn't recommend it. I'm a lot less friendly than you are." The man snorted. "You think you're some bad ass, Isaac?"

"It's Lance, not Isaac. What are we, in the high school locker room? And no, I won't go there. I want her to come to me. I have a jet standing by that will take us back home where she belongs." Alistair felt his temper rise, and when Ally touched him, he pulled her to him.

"She no longer belongs to you," he told the man calmly. "She belongs to me. And you might as well go back home on your jet before that, too, is repossessed."

Keith gave him the thumbs up, and Alistair disconnected the call. He had to take several deep breaths before he was able to ask where the man was. He looked at Ryland, who was talking on his own phone and knew his brother was taking care of the situation. Ally leaned in and nuzzled against his throat.

"You keep that up and we're going to miss dinner." She pulled back when he spoke to her through their link. *"I need*

you. I know that he didn't touch you, but I have the desire to mark you again."

He felt her desire and wanted to tell everyone to get the hell out, but his brothers were helping him right now, and he had to wait. When Ryland cleared his throat, Ally started to pull away, but Alistair wasn't ready to let her go just yet and pulled her tighter.

"He's at the Route Forty Road Side. It's a dive about ten miles from your office. Do you think he knows that?"

"Probably not," Alistair said.

"I want us to wait him out, but as she's your mate, it's up to the two of you."

Alistair looked at Ally. "What do you want to do? Either way he's not going to touch you and he's not taking you from me. We can confront him or just wait. Eventually, he'll come here, I think, when you don't show there."

"I don't want him to come anywhere, but I'd rather it be on our own turf rather than his. That way when we have to kill him, there are fewer witnesses." Ryland burst out laughing. "I was just kidding. I guess you're right. We wait it out. But why didn't you ask him about the other man?"

"He'll just deny that. And besides, when he does come here, we can get what he knows out of him with our secret weapon." Alistair looked at Bronwyn. "He won't know what hit him when she's done with him."

Dinner was called, and they all sat down. Alistair watched as each of them teased her into a less frightened mood, and Bronwyn and Ally made a date for the following afternoon. They were going to target practice in the back yard.

Alistair needed to go to the office in the morning and felt better knowing that Ally was going to be in good hands. He'd been taking some time off because of the shooting, but now he had to return. Things were piling up, and his staff needed him. After dinner, his family left, and he and Ally went to the office where he was going to show her what they had on Isaac.

"I'd rather you marked me again." His body hardened at her words. "You could take me across this desk and bite me if you want."

"Yes." She smiled at him and told him to sit down. He moved to his desk chair and sat down. Adjusting his cock so it wouldn't strangle in his jeans, he watched her walk toward him as she unbuttoned her pants.

"I've thought of some things I'd like to do with you." He nodded. Anything, he'd do anything with her. "I was wondering if I could suck your cock for you."

He pushed his chair back from the desk and nodded. "Come here and you can do whatever you want to me. So long as you remember that I get to return the favor."

"I hope so." She moved between his open tights and went down onto her knees. He watched as she unsnapped his jeans and pulled the zipper down slowly. "I've never done this before, so if I do something wrong will you tell me?"

"From where I'm sitting right now, you can't fail. Christ, you have no idea how much I want you to do this." She nodded and rubbed her cheek over his cloth-covered cock. "Ally, please don't tease me."

"But I love to do this." She nipped at his cock, and he stretched out so that she could get to him better. "You're so hard and thick. I love the feel of you when you're inside of me."

He lifted his hips to help her remove his pants. His boxers came down as well, and his cock strained from his groin to have her touch him. He wrapped his hand around his cock and fisted himself slowly. She leaned in and licked the pearly cum at the tip and moaned.

"Take me, Ally. All of me. Take me into your mouth." She sat up and wrapped her mouth over his dark head, and he moaned. "Christ baby, that's it."

She moved up and down on his cock as she reached beneath his shirt and up to his nipples. They had never been sensitive before, but now it was as if they were directly attached to his cock. He nearly came up off the chair when she pinched him. He wrapped his hand into her hair and told her to lick him.

Her tongue was like a hot slick fire that ignited his blood everywhere she touched him. When she cupped his balls a little too tightly, he gripped her hair. "Careful, love."

She moaned when he showed her how to touch him, and when she lifted her head to the tip again and licked the tiny eye, he held his breath, afraid she was going to stop.

"Will you come down my throat?" He nodded. "I want you to. I want you to fuck me like this until you come."

He cried out when she took him into her mouth again and swallowed him past her throat. Every time she swallowed, he felt her tighten around him until he thought he'd die from pleasure. As soon as she cupped his balls again, he felt his cock jerk.

She took him all. Even as he fucked her, his hips rising up off the seat to go even deeper into her mouth, she moaned, vibrating along his cock until he saw stars. When he pulled her loose, jerking her head up, he stood up and pulled her to her feet. Her pants were nothing but shreds by the time he got her laying on his cleared desk.

He entered her hard and fast. Her body took him like she was made for him. When her legs wrapped around his hips, he reached up and tore the rest of her clothes from her, and then fell on her to take her nipple into his mouth. Her fingers dug deep into his head as he held her, and his cock pounded her so hard he had a hard time keeping her breast in his mouth. When she screamed out her release, he moved up her throat to her shoulder and sank his canines deep into her flesh as he came in her again. He felt her mouth over his own shoulder and commanded her to bite him.

Her teeth tore at his flesh, and he felt her come around him again, her scream muffled against his skin. When she cried out again, he lifted his head and looked down at her. She was his, all his.

"I want you to be with me." She nodded. "I want to change you. I want you to be a cat, like me."

"Yes, please yes. Change me." She tilted her neck, and he licked along the vein. "Please."

He tore at her vein and felt the blood fill his mouth. It was hot and spiked with her heat. Sucking hard, he held her as he tore harder, deeper, leaving his essences in her wound so that he could make her one of them. As her body began to weaken, he touched her mind again.

"Don't fight it, baby. Let my saliva work through you." She moaned, and he knew that she hurt. *"I'm sorry. I should have prepared you more for this, but I couldn't wait."*

"I love you." His heart skipped several beats as he was waiting for her to say more. He then felt the first stirring of her cat. As she emerged, he lifted his head and looked down at her. It was happening, and he was suddenly glad that she was unconscious. It was going to be painful for her for a while.

CHAPTER 7

Lance sat on the messy bed and looked around the room. He had no idea how he was going to pay for the damage he'd caused in here, and right now didn't really care. He was still pissed at that prick who thought that he was better than him. Alistair Golden had always been a sore spot for him.

It had started when they were on a case; on opposite sides, of course, but the case should have been open and shut. Lance had worked some of the angles like he always did, trying to discredit the man on trial, as well as his lawyer. But Alistair had been right on top of things and had him looking like a schoolyard bully before the first witness was called. It was downhill from there.

Lance didn't remember what the trial had even been about other than the man had supposedly robbed some convenience store. Where Lance had relied on police reports and witnesses, Alistair had testimony that stated the suspect was at a school program with his daughter. When Lance had tried to discredit that, saying that with the lights off he could have slipped out, Alistair had provided the program where it stated that the man was in charge of the lighting and had been in full view of nearly fifty people the entire time. Then he'd handed the judge signed affidavits from every one of them, including the class of fourth graders.

The judge looked at Lance like he was a bug under his thumb and he was ready to crush him. "You have anything else there, counselor? Something more than a bunch of the same crap you try at every case you're on? Things sure are different when the lawyer for the other team isn't intimated by you, aren't they?"

"I've won more cases in a month than this one, your honor. I doubt very much this one case is going to make my firm let me go." He laughed a little nervously because he knew they were starting to crack down on him even then. "I'll just mark this one up to bad help and move on with my life."

"You do that. In the meantime, you didn't answer my question. Do you have anything more on this man? If not, I'm going to let it go, too. I'm sure this man wants to move on with his life, as well." Lance nodded and started shoving papers into his brief case. And when the judge dismissed the case, Lance remembered Alistair coming to him with his hand outstretched.

"No hard feelings on this, right?" Lance looked down his nose at the younger man and sneered. Alistair stared at him for several seconds before Lance left him standing there. He would still laugh about it when he thought about it, but now it only pissed him off.

He looked at his watch and tried to remember when he'd called the man. It had been nearly two hours, he knew, so where the hell was she? It wasn't like her not to do as he'd told her. Well, not since he'd hit her the first time. Then she started running. And every time he was able to bring her back and hurt her again. He frowned when he thought of his mom.

She had hit Ally, too; not badly, but enough that her mouth had been swollen when he'd needed her to be at a function with him. And because he was so pissed that she wasn't perfect, he'd hit her a great deal more than he'd meant to. She'd nearly died, and when she went to the hospital, he thought for sure she was going to press charges. He looked at his phone again when it rang.

"They're going to come and take the computer in the morning. I've hidden it away, and they'll never find it, but thought you should know that you're going to have to step this up a bit." He lay back on the bed as his mother continued. "The plane had to come back, too. That idiot pilot of yours turned you in to your firm and now they have taken him on as a client. He's suing your ass as we speak for non-payment of wages. I think the IRS is going to be involved, as well. Something about not paying the taxes you've been taking out of checks."

"I was paying the insurance policy with the money. I was going to pay it back when I got the insurance payoff." Of course, he couldn't tell them that, but he had hoped that by now he would have been able to collect. Allyson was becoming a real pain in the ass.

"Also, you should know that as of a few days ago you are no longer employed with the firm you worked for. Can they fire you like that?" He told her that they could pretty much do what they wanted. "They sent you a letter by courier. I signed for it and read it. You're not even getting your vacation or retirement money. They said they are using them for your legal issues. What legal issues?"

"They said that I stole money from the firm by overbilling and that I hit my secretary." He closed his eyes against the pounding headache that was coming on. "I don't suppose they said what they did with my things, did they? I had some very valuable things on my desk and in my office."

"No, all they said was for you to have a nice day at the end. I can go down there if you'd like and see if I can get it. No one treats my boy like this." He wanted to laugh, but he thought he'd throw up if he did. "Find the fucking bitch and kill her. We'll collect here in Nevada, and no one there will ever know."

But they would. He knew that if she was living with Alistair, she'd told him everything, and he was just slick enough to dig into the other deaths and find whatever he wanted. Alistair had probably already checked with his second wife's dad and found out a great many things the man said he had on him. Lance thought he might be better off putting a bullet in his own head and ending it. But his mother said something that made him sit up.

"What did you just say?" He held his breath while she wound down about him interrupting her again. "Just tell me what the fuck you've done."

"I said I hired some people to get the job done for you. The first one failed miserably, but the man I contacted in the first place said he would find her himself and kill her. It was reasonably easy to figure out where she was, he said. Women like to shop, and he had her picture and all, so he had his men staking the place out. She, sadly, lived, but he promised me that it won't happen again." She laughed, and he felt the skin on his arms dance at the sound. "Of course, he said he has to get her now. He has a reputation to uphold."

"How are you paying him?" She sighed, and he knew that he was going to be pissed. "What have you sold now that we can't really do without?"

"I sold all my furs some time ago, but I lied to you about what I got for them. So I used that as a...I used that as bait. He thinks she stole all your bearer bonds you had locked away, and now we just want her dead. I told him that while we got them back, we still want her to pay. He agreed."

Christ, his mom was hiring hit men without any money. And when they figured it out, she'd be just as dead as Allyson. He wished he had the means to take out a policy on her right now. It would more than likely pay off before Allyson's did. He lay back on the bed again and listened to her prattle on about money and what she was going to do with her share. He could only think that even if he had all the money from the policy in his hands it wouldn't be enough to get him out of this never-ending hole he was in.

He was in for millions. And not only that, he was behind in his taxes for the past nine years. Then there was the loan he'd taken out without anyone knowing…and the man he got it from wouldn't follow any rules but his own. That loan was coming due in two short weeks. He was so fucked.

When his father was alive they'd never had these problems. Money seemed to be right at their fingertips all the time. Then one day his dad had gone into his office, had put a gun under his chin, and pulled the trigger. Apparently, he hadn't been any good with money, either.

He'd left a note stating that he just couldn't say no to his family, and that whatever they wanted he wanted them to have it. He had borrowed so much money against their home that his mom had to move in with him just so she'd not have to live on the streets. His father had made one bad investment after another until there was nothing left. And now Lance was doing the same thing. But he wasn't going to shoot himself and let anyone win over him. He had a plan, and he was going to collect.

"Have you had any luck finding me someone to marry?" She started laughing, and he wondered what he'd missed. When she asked him if he'd been reading the paper, he'd told her that he couldn't afford it. "Just tell me what the fuck is so funny. I need to get out and make my way to Allyson. The people she's staying with told me I could come and get her."

Not entirely true, but he didn't care. Once he got to Alistair's house he was going to collect as much of his things as he could to pawn. Then he was going to use that money to get Allyson on a plane and back in the bosom of his family. Just before he killed her.

"You are no longer a person any woman wants to be near, much less seen with. And what your firm hasn't said about you, Marcus is filling in for them. You're being dragged through the papers as if you've killed someone. I'll be lucky if I can get you a housekeeper rather than a suitable wife."

Lance was going down. It was no longer a matter of *if* but *when*. He had to do something to redeem himself. But without money all he could do was sit back and let the papers have at it. He told his mom he had to go, and simply hung up on her. He had to think and he couldn't with her on the line.

Allyson had caused most of this. The one time he'd lost his temper had ended with her getting a divorce from him, as well as getting her in touch with someone that had a great deal more money than he had, and even more respectability. He had to get her.

Pulling out the phonebook that had seen better days, he looked up Alistair's address. But according to the nice little map that was provided in the stupid thing, he lived far enough away from where he was it might well have been China. He started to close it when he saw the address of his offices. That was a good deal closer. He decided to pay a visit to his old friend's office first thing in the morning. Things were about to change, he thought. Change for the better, he hoped.

~~~

Ally felt as if her entire body was on fire. She sat up in bed and looked around at what was burning her. She looked at Alistair, who was sleeping in the chair next to the bed. She wondered what had happened. Then she remembered.

He'd bitten her and changed her. She lifted her arm above her head and looked at it. She thought her skin looked firmer, her muscle tone much tighter. Stretching out her fingers she thought about claws and felt the first tingle of something moving along her tips. She shoved her hand under the blanket quickly.

"You'll be sore for a few days. Nothing major, but there will be times when you'll feel it more than others. Like in your legs and lower back." She looked at him as he stared at her.

"Why there? I mean, why my legs and lower back?" He told her he didn't know. "Have you ever done this before?"

"No. I've seen it done, but I never did it myself." He sat up and looked at her. "Are you sore?"

She moved her legs and felt the muscles protest…not badly, but like she'd walked a great deal and without a lot of preconditioning. She told him she was fine. When she sat up, her back did hurt, and she moaned before she could stop it. He was beside her before she could ask for help.

"When you stand hold on to me. You're going to be dizzy from the loss of blood." He helped her to stand and stood with her as the room seemed to move back and forth. She smiled at him when he paled. "You're going to be all right."

"Of course I am. You're here, right?" She let him take her to the bathroom, but made him wait in the bedroom while she peed. They were sleeping together, but there was a line that just didn't get crossed.

When she came out, she felt much better. Her back hurt a little, but she knew it was nothing that a hot bath wouldn't help. She opened the door only to find herself alone in the room. She turned on the water, went back, and stripped down.

Her body looked toned, too. The scars that she had from the one time Lance had hit her hard enough to nearly kill her seemed to have faded, and she had to search hard for the one that had marred her lip. She was looking for other scars when he knocked on the door.

"I have to see you." She heard the little bit of fear in his voice and opened the door immediately. "I was worried you'd hurt yourself or fell. Are you really okay?"

"Yes. I feel great." She stretched her arms over her head and watched the hunger in his eyes. "Would you like for me to show you?"

"Christ. I wish I could, I really do, but I have to be to work this morning. I have…. Fuck it." He tore off his tie and picked her up. "This is not going to be what I wanted to do to you the first time I took you as a cat."

She moaned and it turned to a purr when he stoked her back with his fingers. She let him sit her on the counter as he pulled open his pants. When she reached for him, he took both her hands and put them on the counter.

"You will have to forgive me, baby, but I need you now." His cock slid into her even as his pants fell to the floor. She was so ready for him that she nearly came when he took her nipple.

She tightened her legs around his waist when he picked her up and lifted her up and down over him. When the wall touched her back, he took her mouth hard, his tongue sliding along hers and taking possession of her mouth. When he slid his mouth along her chin to her collarbone, she moaned again. He was taking her so hard against the wall she wondered if it would support them. Digging her nails deep into his back, she heard him snarl, and knew that his cat was coming to the surface.

"He wants her. Let her come out for him." Alistair's voice was harsh, gravelly almost. Her cat seemed to be so close that she was afraid of losing her. "Let her go. I've got you both."

The cat in her seemed to scream to the surface. Ally felt her cat's body roll over her human one and watched as Alistair's cat did the same. Fur and stripes seemed to race quickly along his neck and arms. His face seemed to stretch and expand even as his eyes went from the warm brown to a golden hue. His teeth stretched in his mouth, and she felt hers do the same, and as soon as he bit her, she bit him back and felt the bond with the cats fall into place. As soon as she felt it, her body exploded in the hardest climax she'd ever had.

Vaguely she heard Alistair roar, his body slamming into hers so hard that she knew that she'd be sore for a long while. Walking would be difficult. But even as that thought occurred to her, he lifted his head and looked at her.

"Come. Come again and take my throat." She felt as if a trigger had been pulled and she came again, her body bowed from the wall as her cat roared from her. When she saw Alistair's throat exposed, she leaned in and sank her teeth so deep into his throat the blood didn't just pour from the wound but gushed in long streams down the back of her throat. Tearing at the skin, she knew that she'd marked him, just as he'd done to her.

They climaxed together, both of them falling over the edge of the cliff and never looking back. Even as she tried to hold on to the sensations, she knew that for as long as she lived, this would be the one memory that would live forever. She felt the air around her tighten, and then she, too, shifted behind him. Christ, they'd torn up the room.

When he lifted his head after she sealed the wound, Ally could see that his cat was still close. She wanted to ask him if hers was there, as well, when she felt her purr along her insides. She looked at Alistair when he laughed.

"I can feel her, too. She's well satisfied, as is my cat." He licked along her throat, which had her purring again. "You have any idea what that sound does to me?"

"Yes. When you do it, I feel it all the way to my toes." She looked at the steam-covered mirror over the counter. "I'm betting that we have very little hot water left."

She stepped in to take a quick shower, and he came in after her. When he washed her hair, she helped him with his back. Licking along the small scratches she'd put there, he told her she was going to kill him. Laughing, they stepped out and heard his phone ringing.

"It's my secretary. She wants to know where the hell I am." He answered the phone while she got dressed. He was joking with the person on the other end and telling whoever it was it had been her fault. She stuck her tongue out at him as he pulled on another shirt.

"She'll think I had my way with you and that's why you're late." He grinned. "She already does, doesn't she?"

"Yes. Mary Margaret is a cat, as well. There are many of them that work in my office. I try to help them get a foot in the door so that when they go out on their own they'll know how to work around what they are. Some people...most people...still don't believe we exist. And that's probably a good thing." He kissed her mouth gently. "You are going to be okay now. You know that, right?"

"Yes. I was...last night I didn't care what you did to me so long.... No, that's not right. I did care. I wanted this very badly. I want you very badly." She took his tie from him, put it around his neck, and tied it for him as she thought about what she was. He lifted her chin and looked at her.

"You told me you loved me. Do you?" She nodded. "Say it for me. I want to hear you say it to me again."

"I love you. I'm not sure how it happened after I had closed my heart so tightly. But I do love you." He kissed her again.

"And I love you." He backed up two steps. "But if I stay here much longer, I will never get to work and there are clients waiting on me to keep them out of jail."

He was nearly out the door when he came back and kissed her again. She laughed as he growled low at her and moved out the door again just as Jed was coming in. He beeped the horn just as she was closing the door.

"A package is coming for you today. It's your cell phone. I hope you don't mind. I wanted you to have it in case you wanted to send me dirty pictures or call me. It should be ready to go with numbers programmed in it already." She nodded. "And don't forget that Bronwyn is coming over today. She said around noon. Probably lunch time, if I know her."

He finally pulled away, and she watched him. When she turned back to the kitchen, she realized this was the first time since the mall shooting that she'd been without him near her. She looked at Jed, who was smiling at her.

"Congratulations." She looked at him blankly. "You're a cat now, too. How are you feeling? Hungry? Out of sorts?"

"Yes," she answered, and he laughed.

CHAPTER 8

Alistair was deep in a file when his secretary knocked. He looked up at her, and her frown had him standing. When she shut the door behind her, he thought maybe it was his family again. Keith had been flirting with her for weeks now, and she probably had enough. Then he remembered that Bronwyn and Ally were on the shooting range in the backyard.

Before he could let that terrify him, she spoke. "There's a Mr. Isaac here to see you. He doesn't have an appointment, and he's…he said you knew he was supposed to see you today." He sat back down in his chair and stared at her. "You want me to make him an appointment and have him come back?"

He started to nod, then decided to get this over with. "Contact Brock. I think he's still here. Have him come see me. Once he's here, let the man in. And Mary Margaret, don't let him speak to Brock, either. We're going to play this game my way."

She smiled at him and started to open the door. "I'll assume that you're going to need security to escort him out, so I'll have them here. This is going to be fun, isn't it?"

He nodded and smiled. She was smiling as well when she stepped out. Clearing off his desk, he called Ryland and let him know what was going on.

"You need anyone there with you?" He told him Brock was coming. "Good. I don't trust that he'd say you did something to him and try to sue you. There are a few things coming in here that you should know about. That judge that helped Ally called back. He's willing to sign anything you need to have this bastard put behind bars."

"I'll call him when this prick is gone." Brock came in after a sharp knock. "Brock is here to kick his ass if I need him. I'll let you know what happened after he leaves. Is Ally all right?"

"She and Bronwyn just came in for lunch. Bronwyn said she really is a great shot, and you should also know that she's doing really well with other things, as well." He'd forgotten to tell Ryland what he'd done. "You do know that all changes are supposed to be cleared through me before you do them, right?"

"I was...we were...." He took a deep breath. "We got caught up in the moment, and I needed to change her."

Ryland didn't say anything for several seconds, and the door opened. When Ryland did speak, Alistair couldn't tell if he was mad or not. He told him they'd discuss it when he had more time. Then he simply hung up.

"Hello. I was hoping to meet with you alone." Alistair offered Isaac a seat as the man continued. "You do know who I am, correct?"

"Yes. You're the man who thinks I'm going to give over the woman I love for no other reason than you think I should. But I should tell you now it's not going to happen. She and I are in love." Alistair watched as Isaac tried to regain control of his temper, but he couldn't help but to needle him more.

"Has this anything to do with your current finances? I've heard that you have some major catching up to do."

Brock sat down next to Isaac, and Alistair had to bite his lip to keep from laughing. Brock was a big man, and he could be intimidating as hell when he wanted to be. Apparently, now was one of those times. He even scooted his chair closer to Isaac just to crowd him.

"Do you mind?" Brock shrugged, then looked at him and winked. Alistair thought maybe he was doing this to make him lose his cool, and it seemed to be working. "I think we got off on the wrong foot. I just wanted to speak to her to see that she's all right and to see if she'd consider coming back with me for a little while. To see if we can work out our differences, and…my mother misses her. She'd never had a daughter before, and she and Allyson got along so well that now that she's not there, she's sad."

Alistair watched him look at his hand several times and realized that the idiot had made notes. He was reading from notes on his hand. When he looked at Brock again, he knew his brother had seen them, as well.

"I can ask her, but I'm pretty sure she's going to tell you *no*. She and I are planning our wedding right now and fixing up the house for the two of us. She's very satisfied." He knew that the man got the double meaning because he looked at him like he wanted to hit him. "And she loves my family, as well. I have five brothers and a sister-in-law."

"I would really like to talk to her. Privately. She and I have some unfinished business that we need to settle, and once that's done then she can—"

"You didn't answer me before. Does this have anything to do with your finances?" Isaac looked at him sharply. "The reason I ask is she told me that you were having some major issues, and I heard from a friend of mine out west that you'd been terminated from your firm. That's gotta suck."

He stood so suddenly that Brock growled low. Alistair had a few seconds to wonder if Brock was going to attack when Isaac started to pace. He was mumbling to himself, but he could hear him.

"Stupid cunt is more trouble than she's almost worth. Why did I think this was going to work? And what the fuck did I think she was going to do? Come down here and let me kill her?" Isaac turned to him when a growl spilled from his lips. "Did you just growl at me?"

"Growl? Don't be ridiculous." Alistair looked at Brock. "Did you hear anything? I swear these buildings now days.... Look, Isaac, sit down and tell us why you're really here. I will tell you this, that you're not coming within a foot of Ally, and even if you tried, I think you'd be surprised at her now. She's not the same woman who left you."

"I think I'd know my wife a little better than you would. How long have you two been dating? A couple of weeks? We were married for years before she got it into her head to run, and I want her back. Today. She's been fucking around enough. Call the bitch and have her get her skinny ass down here now."

Alistair nodded to Brock, and he stood up, went to the door, and opened it. Five guards walked in. Alistair knew that three of them were wolves who would not take kindly to someone pissing off their boss. Brock stood in front of them with his arms crossed over his chest.

"You can leave with these gentlemen, or you can leave by the window behind you. Either way works for me. And if you doubt my ability to toss you out, you're as stupid as Ally says you are." Brock let a little of his cat go, just enough to let his canines show. Isaac backed up and bumped into the window.

"You can't just do that. You can't just threaten a man and expect to get away with it." Isaac looked at Alistair. "Aren't you going to call him off? Are you just going to sit there and let him do this to me?"

"Absolutely. I might even try and do it myself." He looked at the guard and told them to show him out. Just before they touched him, Alistair stood up. "And you should know that what my brother is telling you isn't going to be anything compared to what I'll do to you if you come near Ally again. Do I make myself perfectly clear?"

Isaac jerked from Stan Flores, his head of security, and glared at him. "You've not heard the last from me. She belongs to me, and I need her to come home with me now. There are things going on that—"

"Take him out and toss him into the street." As he was pulled from the office screaming that he was going to sue, Brock went with them. Alistair wasn't sure that was a good idea but didn't care what happened to Isaac at that point. With the door shut, Alistair reached for Ally.

"You should have seen the look on Bronwyn's face when I shot the bull's-eye six times out of six. She said I was near perfect." He smiled, knowing that he needed this more than he'd thought. *"And she's teaching me how to fight. So don't be surprised when you see that I have a black eye."*

"She hit you in the eye?" His cat seemed to take exception to that. *"Tell her I'm going to kick her ass—"*

She was laughing. He leaned back in his chair and let the phone settle back into the cradle. He hadn't even realized he'd reached for it until then. He was on the verge of calling his sister-in-law and telling her off. Ally was still laughing when she told him she was kidding.

"You dork. She only knocked me on my ass a few times, that's all. Man, she's really strong." She paused, and he

knew she was a little afraid. *"She said that you might be in trouble for changing me without asking for permission. How did she figure it out?"*

"She can smell you. Everyone can. Ryland and I are going to have a talk about it tonight. I should have asked before I changed you." He smiled when she laughed. *"What is it?"*

"I don't think that's going to happen the way he'd planned. I think...well, he said something to me and I sort of snapped at him. I don't think he's very happy with me right now. I said to him...well, he won't assume things about me again."

He wished he could have been there to see that, but was afraid that Ryland would take his anger out on his mate. He started to tell her to back off when Brock came back in the room. He looked entirely too pleased with himself.

"I have to see what Brock has done. I'll talk to you later. I should be home around five. Would you like to have dinner here in town? I can have Jed bring you in."

"Nah, I've been making requests to Jed all day. He's putting together a menu for me. He said I'm more fun to cook for than you. He said you simply say whatever he has is fine. I'm telling him what I want. We're having steaks on the grill and something that we've been tweaking." He felt she was talking to someone else and waited. *"You and I are going to shift, right? I'm excited about that."*

"I'm going to shift with you. Then I'm going to take you in the woods, and I don't mean to simply take you into the wooded area. I mean I'm going to take you. Several times." He felt her blush. *"Christ, I have to get back to work or I'll be here late. I love you."*

She told him she loved him more, and closed the connection. He looked at Brock, who was still smiling. There was something very evil about that smile.

"He's mad at us…not that I care, but he's also going to send you the bill for his dry cleaning. I might have roughed him up a little, and he fell."

Alistair looked out the window. It was pouring rain, and he knew that when it rained this hard there was a large puddle outside the building. He leaned back in his chair and regarded his brother.

"He won't stop, will he?" Brock shook his head. "The only way to make him go away is either prison or death. I'm not opposed to killing him, but I don't want to go to jail, either."

"You won't have to if he keeps up like he is." Brock took out a cigar and put it in his mouth. He didn't light it, because he knew that there was no smoking in the building, but he knew that he wanted to. It was Brock's one vice when he was pissed off.

"I want to double up on the security around here. And at the house. Probably all of them. We'll even get someone from our team at Jules's place, both the apartment and his studio." Brock told him he'd already taken care of it. "I got Ally a phone, and I had a tracking device put on it, too. She doesn't know it, but I was afraid for her."

"She won't be alone. I think she and Bronwyn have hit it off pretty good, and Mom already loves her, too. She's got a great head on her shoulders and knows him better than we do. She's not going to be stupid."

Alistair nodded. "I changed her. Last night, she and I…I asked her, and she wanted it too. We're going to see how she likes shifting in the outdoors when I get home."

"Ryland told me." Alistair wanted to ask what he'd said but wasn't sure he wanted to know. "When we were dealing with dick weed, he told me that Ally came into his office and ripped into him. She said that she had made you change her and that if he had a problem with it, he was going to have to deal with her and she was pretty sure she could take him."

Alistair could see her doing that and laughed. "I bet that made his day. Did he tell you what else she said?"

Brock nodded. "She also told him that if he said one negative word to you about it she was going to put something in his food the next time he ate and he'd be limp-dicked for a month. Of course, he didn't tell her that those kinds of drugs don't work on us, but he said she was so full of fire that he was afraid she'd make him limp for the rest of his life. He said she's a frightening little bitch when she wants to be."

Alistair was proud of her and couldn't help but think about when she'd told him and his mom that she couldn't say things like that. He laughed and told Brock about it. He was laughing when his phone rang.

"My name is Marcus Cook. I think I spoke to your brother a couple of weeks ago. You may not know me, but I think we might have a common enemy in Lance Isaac."

Brock left the office as Alistair sat up higher in his seat. "Yes, Mr. Cook. He just left my office as a matter of fact. He was here trying to convince me that he's a loving husband who wants his wife back."

"Allyson? She's a good girl. I met her once, though I doubt she'd remember. It was a long time before she met the ass who murdered my daughter." Alistair didn't caution the man on slander because he was pretty sure that man was right. "I've finally gotten the court order I need to have her body exhumed and autopsied. Could be telling, I think."

If it was, there were going to be all sorts of repercussions for Isaac to try and get out of. "Does Isaac know about this? If he does, he might skip the country. I understand he still has a jet that he could use."

"The firm where he worked took that yesterday for legal fees. There is some story going around that he hit his secretary and that he took some money. Overbilling, I understand." Alistair told him that was true. "He's not going to have a pot to piss in when I finish with him. He's been having my daughter's hospital bills sent here instead of paying them off. I've also made it so he's not getting any insurance from her, either, not with me saying she's been murdered and all. I think he poisoned her for her money."

As much as Alistair wanted to tell him he agreed, he knew he was in no position to say it. For all he knew, the man could be fishing for information to use against him, as well. He only told the man how sorry he was for his loss.

"She was a wonderful girl, Mr. Golden. Just wonderful. And she had fallen for the ass because he said all the right words to her. I shouldn't have let her go through with it. I blame myself for her death every day." The man broke down, and Alistair waited. It would be hard, he knew, to lose someone. But a child would be devastating.

"Mr. Cook, my family and I are going to meet tonight to discuss this thing with Isaac. We're afraid for what he might do to Ally if he keeps at this. He threatened me and my family today if we didn't hand her over to him."

Alistair hoped that his family wouldn't mind having a meeting on such short notice, and he was sure that Ally would forgive him for their run, but this was getting to a critical point, and he was afraid for all of them.

"I can do that. I can...you sure you don't mind me coming, too?" He told him no. "I might have some information that will help you. I understand you're an attorney, a good one, too."

"I'm an attorney, but a good one? I suppose. I love what I do." Alistair cleared his throat. "I'm in love with Ally, Mr. Cook. She and I are going to be married as soon as it can be arranged. And I'm not going to let anything happen to her."

"I can tell that." Alistair heard him speaking to someone else. Then he came back on the phone. "I can be there this evening. If you give me the address, I'll have a car bring me around. Can you recommend a good hotel?"

"I can do that. I'll set everything up on this end, and if you tell me what time you'll be landing, I'll even have a car there to bring you to my house." Cook told him he would be there around four. "I'll have everything set up, and I hope you like home cooking, because my cook has been playing with some recipes with Ally, and it should be interesting."

Cross laughed. "It's been a while, but I would love to have a home-cooked meal. I'll see you tonight. And thank you."

He called home first and talked to Jed. He said that the *little tiger* was in the shower. He then asked if he would like for him to have her call him. Alistair laughed at the nickname and wondered if Ally knew about it yet.

"Yes. Tell her about the company. Also, tell her he's expecting a home-cooked meal. Do you mind helping with that?" He laughed. "I suppose we should entertain more, but I've never wanted to before."

"She'll be good for this house, I think. I'll see what she wants to have and then have her call you. I need to go into the store for some things. Would it be all right if the little tiger went with me? I'll take care of her."

"I know you will. Please don't let her stay there alone. I don't trust that idiot to not to try something. If she doesn't want to go with you, then…then drop her off at Ryland's house. I'll explain if she gets upset."

Then he called Ryland. "Cross says he might have some information that might help us. He…you should have heard him, Ryland. The man is devastated to have lost his child."

"I would be, as well. The meeting is a great idea, and even if the man doesn't have anything we don't already have, it might do him some good to have some people around that he knows are going to do something. And we will."

"I know," he told Ryland. "I wanted to talk to you about my changing Ally. I should have—"

"Don't. I had a long talk with her and Bronwyn. And you can't guess who was more pissed at me. I'm telling you that that mate of yours can tear a hide off anything. And here I thought she'd be lucky if she didn't crumble at the first sign of trouble." He laughed. "You're fine. I mean it, and with the way things are going, it might save her life to be able to shift and have the extra strength. Bronwyn said I should have congratulated you, not made you feel like shit about it. I am sorry about that."

"Thank you, Ryland. You have no idea what it means to me that you said that." After Ryland said he'd make sure everyone was at his house at five, they hung up. Alistair decided he had a great family and was gladder for them every day. He dug into his work and managed to finish up in time to go to the airport to get Mr. Cook.

CHAPTER 9

Lance sat in his hotel room, too tired to think about what had happened. He'd had it all worked out and knew that he'd eventually have the man eating out of his hands. He looked at his hand where he'd given himself notes and wondered at what point he'd lost control of the situation. He thought it had been when that other man kept edging closer to him, but was sure that was only part of it. Lance hadn't even gotten to the part of his speech were he told Alistair that he was still in love with his wife and wanted her to come back. At least he didn't think he had.

Pacing the small confines of the room, he tried to ignore how dirty his trousers were and the mud that caked his shoes. He knew that they had cost a great deal more than he'd ever paid for a pair of shoes. And now they were ruined. The filth would never come out of them. And why did the large man have to knock him into the puddle in the first place?

"He's going to pay for that, too." He kicked off the shoes and put them into the trash. There was no way he was ever going to put them on again. They would be a constant reminder of what had just happened. And he was no closer to getting her back than he was before.

He glared at his cell phone, knowing that even if he wanted to call his mother, there was no way to do it. The thing had been shut off last night, right in the middle of a call to get a pizza delivered. And he was still pissed about that, too. It had never shown up, and he'd had to walk to the convenience store five blocks away only to find out it was closed. He was sick to death of nothing going his way. When his phone rang, he nearly fell back from it.

"I could only pay the first past due amount, and have to come up with the rest by the end of the week or it's off for good. Have you managed to get anything done on your end?" His mother never said *hello*, he just realized, but launched into whatever she had called about before anyone else could speak. "Lance, are you listening to me? We have to get his cleared up before everything else comes down on our heads."

"I went to speak to the people she's staying with, and the man is a brute. He and his brothers told me that if I came near her, they'd hurt me." He snorted, though he was sure that hurt was nothing compared to whatever they had planned for him. "I'm going to see if I can get to his house today and have a few words with my wife. She's been fucking around with me long enough."

"I think you should just kill her when you see her." She paused. "Never mind. You'd just fuck that up as well. I want you to come home. I've been looking into what it would cost for you to fly back here, and I've just enough to get you here. That man I was telling you about said he has a good lead on her and he'll have this completed by the end of the week. He is giving us a discount, too, because of the way it was handled before."

He didn't want to leave this in the hands of someone else. He wanted to take care of it. And if the man knew about this, then what was to say he wouldn't tell someone for more money? He had represented people like him, and knew what they were about.

"I'm not coming home until I speak to Allyson. I want to know why the cunt ran. And I know it has nothing to do with me hitting her. She enjoyed that entirely too much for that to be it."

He grinned when he thought of her cowering in the corner when he'd stood over her, and wanted to feel that power again. Then have sex with her. He loved the feeling of dominating her after he'd knocked her around, and only getting to do it the few times had only whet his appetite for more.

"You get yourself arrested and you're on your own. I don't have anything left to sell. Not after yesterday." He was almost afraid to ask and didn't have to when she started to tell him. "The computer people came with the police. And since they couldn't find the computer, they had the right to take anything in the room of equal value. I handed over the computer, but right behind him were the credit card people. They took everything that wasn't nailed down. This is getting out of hand. That girl has caused us enough problems. Take care of it or I will."

He closed his eyes, ignoring her threat. "Did they find the safe?" He knew from her laughter that they'd not only found it but had gotten it opened as well.

"They knew the combination. I'm betting that cunt you married before Allyson gave it to someone, and that's all they needed. Took everything in it, including the cash you had stashed in it. How could you hide that from your mother?" He wanted to tell her because she would spend it on stupid shit like her hair when he needed it for his collection, but said nothing as she continued. "Your suits are gone, as well as your shoes and cufflinks. They said we still owe them a great deal more, and they are going to come for the cars today. Those were your father's."

He had figured that someone would remember the cars sooner or later, but had hoped he'd be able to sell them before that happened. He sat down when she told him that the police were guarding them so that she couldn't even go out to the garage and look at them one last time.

"They're afraid you'll run off in one of them." He laughed, and it sounded manic even to his own ears. "I don't think they realize that you've never driven a car in your life and wouldn't know the first thing about taking off in them."

"This is not funny, young man. You're supposed to take care of your mother, not bring her down like your father did. I'm not enjoying this."

"Neither am I." He got up to pace again and realized now if they cleaned out his safe and anyone bothered to look at some of the things in it, he was as good as dead. He had been keeping notes on everything since he'd been a child, and when he'd gotten to be an adult, nothing had changed. He had so many things in those journals that even one of them would have him strapped to a table as they filled his body with poison. Murder using poison as well as the murder of a minor were just a few things that they now had him for.

"I can't come home. If I do, they'll arrest me as soon as I get off the plane...assuming I even get that far." He decided he might as well, if nothing else, be honest with her. "You need to get as far away as possible. Change your name, everything about you, because if they find you after reading those journals, you're going down with me. Your help alone in getting me the stuff for Paula is going to get you a long stay in a federal prison."

"What have you done?" He laughed again, terror running through his body hot and heavy. "I will not go to prison because you have a spending problem, and I had nothing to do with the poison you fed to that woman to kill her off. Nothing! Do you hear me?"

He hung up and sat on the bed. He was going to make her pay. Allyson caused all this because she ran and wouldn't do what he'd told her. He wasn't stupid enough to think he was ever going to collect on the insurance now, but he was going to kill her. Her and that fucking bastard she was living with. He went to the bathroom and took a long, hot shower. Then naked, he lay down on the bed and covered up. Closing his eyes, he let his mind drift over what he had to do, and hoped to Christ he was able to get one thing to go his way for a change.

~~~

The jet landed without a hitch. While Alistair had money and a great deal of it, he'd never considered the purchase of a jet to make his life easier. The few times he'd had to fly somewhere he'd simply booked the cheapest flight he could get and left, not worrying overly much about how he got to his destination. This man, Marcus Cook, reeked of wealth.

"Mr. Cook. I hope your flight was fine?" Cook nodded and smiled but kept turning back toward the tarmac. "I have a car here for us, and we can either go by your hotel or we can go straight to my house."

The second person who walked toward them was an older man who looked to be in his late seventies. But the closer he got to him the older he seemed to get. Cook introduced him as his dad.

"My dad has been helping me with this all along. Dad, this is the young man I was telling you about. Alistair Golden, my father, Troy Cook." They shook hands.

Troy Cook was one of the sharpest attorneys that had ever graduated from Harvard Law. He'd been someone that

Alistair had admired since he'd been a teenager and had seen him on the news talking about a case he'd just won.

"I've read about you. Well, I've had you looked into. You're a sharp young man. Are you going to help my son take this prick out?" Alistair nodded. "Good. He needs someone like you in his corner when this goes to trial."

"I won't be able to go to trial for him, sir." Alistair flushed when the man raised a brow at him. "I don't have a license to practice law in Nevada. I'm assuming that's where this will be held." This time Troy nodded. "I can help him, but that's all I'll be able to do."

"We'll see about that." Alistair had no time to ask him what he meant about that as their luggage was being brought toward them. There was a great deal of it, too…more than a couple of nights' stay worth.

They decided to be dropped off at his house, and then have the driver check them into the hotel and deliver their luggage there, as well. It would be late, Troy told him, and he would not want to carry his things up after the exhausting evening. Alistair doubted this man had ever carried anything more than his wallet for decades, but didn't say anything.

They pulled up in front of his home just as Ryland and Bronwyn did. He introduced them, and Marcus marveled at how lovely Bronwyn looked in the bloom of her pregnancy. Alistair waited for her to say something smart, but she only nodded and thanked him. She turned back to him after they were moving toward the house. Then he nearly burst out laughing when she turned and stuck her tongue out at him. That was the Bronwyn he knew and loved.

He pulled Ally into his arms the moment he saw her. She held him tightly to her, and he could feel her fear. He introduced her to the gentlemen, and she led them to the living room. He was glad to see his mom and the rest of his family there waiting for them. And Keith already had his computer set up.

"I'd like to suggest we table this discussion until after we eat, if you don't mind." Ryland looked around the room as he continued. "If it's okay with everyone else, I'd very much like to have a nice, calm dinner with you. Then we can sit down to business."

"What a capitol idea. A nice, quiet dinner with new friends sounds great. Don't you think, Dad?" Marcus looked at his dad and smiled. "Dad, what is it?"

"You're not human." The breath that he'd been holding seemed to strangle him, and Alistair didn't know what to say to the older Cook. "I thought you were something else when I saw you, but all of you together make me think it more. What are you? Wolf? Something else?"

"Tiger." Troy looked at him and nodded. "All of us are, as is Ally now. We're purebreds. We...how did you know?"

"I'm not nearly as old and stupid as some would have you believe." He glanced at his son as he continued. "I have a housekeeper that's a panther. She didn't tell me. I know you have rules about that. But one night, I was in my yard, and she...well, she kept me from a burglar that was bent on taking what I had. After it was over, she sat down with me and told me what she was. She taught me how to tell when I was around others like her."

Alistair watched as Marcus sat down hard and looked around the room. Troy went to stand next to him and nodded to Ryland. There was a wealth of words said in that simple gesture, and Alistair looked around the room and at Ally. She stepped forward and took Troy's hand.

"I'm happy that you came today. We have some information that I think you might need, but like Ryland said, we should eat first. I've been having a good time in the kitchen today. Our cook, Jed, is an amazing man." Their voices faded as she led the two men into the dining room.

"Do you think he'll tell anyone?" His mom looked at all of them before she looked directly at him. "He could ruin us if he wanted to."

"He won't." He had no idea why he knew that to be true, but he was positive that the Cooks would say nothing. "I think they're more interested in justice for their daughter and granddaughter than they are our family secret."

Ryland nodded. "I think he's right. I think he just wants to make sure that no one else dies by this bastard."

They entered the dining room just as Ally was telling them about her gun practice. The men were charmed by her, Alistair could tell, and they all sat down just as Jed brought out the first tray filled with salad and bread sticks. As they each filled their bowls, conversation started to loosen and become friendlier. By the time dessert was served, they were good friends and a great deal less worried about what they might or might not be. As they went back to the living room, Keith sat down at his computer while Brock handed around files.

"I've had a trace put on the two cell phones on the Isaac account since the first time he called Alistair. He has only called one number other than a couple of pizza places, and those calls have been to the other name on the account…his mother, Aida Isaac. She has called a great many more people, and…okay, I'll get to that in a minute."

Alistair opened his file, and the first thing he saw was a picture of a lovely young woman. Keith nudged him, and he stood up. He'd forgotten they had a plan in the way they were going to explain what they had. Laughing, he stood.

"Sorry. I'm a little nervous. The woman in the first picture is Delia Fry, first wife to Isaac. She was murdered in a restaurant about ten years ago, after only about six months of marriage to Isaac. She had filed for divorce from him two mornings before she was killed. There has been no evidence linking him to her death, but there has been speculation." The second picture was of these men's child. "Paula Cook was married to Isaac for nearly five years before she died. But a great deal of that was while she was in a coma. Her death was marked as suicide, but from what I was told today, that may no longer be the case."

"I've gotten the okay to have her body exhumed and an autopsy performed," Marcus said as he took over the story. "When she died in the hospital all those months ago, they said that there was no reason for one and refused to give one to me. I had hoped to prove that she was murdered, and hope that I'll be proven right when she's checked out."

"My granddaughter would never have killed herself. I don't care what sort of shape they think she was in. I think he gave her something to make all her organs fail like they did. There are several drugs that can do that, and I'm hoping they'll find one of them in her."

"Her liver and kidneys were failing, and they said the pain would have been horrific." Marcus pulled out a handkerchief and wiped at his eyes as he continued. "She told me that she was thinking she'd made a mistake in marrying that bastard, and that she needed my help in divorcing him before she found herself shot like his first wife. It wasn't until after she was in the coma that we discovered that the Isaacs were broke and getting broker by the day. They wanted her money, and when I wouldn't release it to them, he...." He looked at Ally.

"He married me." He nodded. "I had him sign a pre-nup. He wasn't happy about it, but he did it. It was that or I was never going to marry him, especially after he'd hit me. My mother said I was making it look as if I didn't expect our marriage to work out, but after she died I didn't care any longer. And the third time he hit me, I'd had enough and filed for divorce the same day."

"Wait. Are you telling me that he married them for their money?" His mom looked around the room. "That's…. What does he do? Look for some rich single woman and marry her, kill her off, and then inherit her livelihood? That's not right, is it? Please tell me that I misunderstood."

Keith shook his head and stood up. He handed everyone several sheets of paper and looked around the room. "That's not only right, Mom, but it's much worse. He takes out huge insurance policies on them. Then kills them. He has done it twice now. And what I just handed you is a sort of confession that his mom is helping him."

"The mother fucker." Alistair looked at Marcus, thinking the man had said it perfectly. Lance Isaac was a monster.

CHAPTER 10

She tried to sit still, but every time she did something else would pop into her head and make her get up to pace. Lance had told her that he'd taken out a policy on her, and had told her that she should simply tear up the pre-nup and believe that he loved her. She had told him that she would and was glad now that she'd never done it. Not that she thought she ever would.

"He's not going to get you, love." She looked at Alistair as he sat on the couch. His family and the Cooks had left over an hour ago. "He's going to try, but he's not going to get to you."

"I almost wish he would try." She shivered at what she said. "I didn't mean that. I don't want to hurt him, but I do want him out of our lives."

"So do I. And what he said to his mother on the phone was incriminating…even though we can't use it in a court of law, we still use it." She nodded at him. "What else, Ally? What is really bothering you?"

"He was going to kill me. He was going to simply murder me for my money." He reached for her, and she pulled away. "He'll come for you now. You said so yourself that he'll come because he's pissed and afraid. I want you to let me leave you so that you—"

She backed up when he was suddenly in front of her. "You're not leaving me, Ally. Not now, not ever. I love you, and I can't let you go. We'll work this out together. We'll win against him."

She let him pull her into his arms, but she was afraid. He held her for several minutes before she spoke, and when he laughed, she wanted to slug him.

"I don't think this is funny. I just wanted us to have a nice sex-filled evening, and now he's fucking that up, too. If he were here right now, I'd change into a big tiger and tear his dick off." Alistair laughed harder, and she joined him. "I'm sorry. But damn it, what does he think he can gain now? Nothing. I've already spoken to my lawyer, and everything is settled."

He lifted her chin and looked down at her. "What have you settled? If you've given Isaac money, I will blister your ass so hard that you won't be able—"

"No. I didn't…I wouldn't give him the time of day. No, you have it. I mean, you have what I have. It's not as much as you already have, but it's a nice, tidy sum."

"I don't need your money, Ally. I have—" She hit him in the belly. "What the hell was that for?"

His laughter made her know that she'd not hurt him, but she was still pissed. "Why is it our money when it belongs to you, and when it's mine you don't want it? Hum? Is there something wrong with me wanting to contribute to our household?"

"No. But…." She glared, and he stopped. "Okay, how's this? I'd love to add your money to our money."

"Was that so hard?" He leaned in and nipped at her shoulder, and she felt her eyes roll to the back of her head.

There was something so arousing about him biting her like that.

"No, but I am." He rocked into her, and she moaned. "I was wondering if you'd like to go outside, so I can watch you shift. All I've thought about all day is what you're going to look like as my little cat."

"I'm a little afraid. When we did it this morning, I was so wrapped up in having you inside of me that I didn't think about it, but now...." He licked along her throat, and she stepped back from him. "We're not going to make it outside if you keep that up."

Laughing, he took her hand, and the two of them went out the kitchen door, telling Jed they were going to be out late. She had convinced the man to stay on the property from now on, telling him that she liked having him close. The house that had been built for that purpose was perfect for him. He'd told her he'd stay until things were settled. She planned to make sure he stayed forever.

Once outside, all her nerves went on high alert. She was going to change into something not herself and then have Alistair chase her and run her down. When he held her, she knew that he was calming her; she could feel his excitement, and she was afraid of disappointing him.

"If you don't want to do this, we don't have to. You'll be a cat for the rest of your life, and nothing has to happen tonight." She believed him, too. Not just about the cat part...she knew that was the truth. But the part that he didn't care if she didn't want to shift. She looked up at him.

"I love you. Very much." He kissed her gently on the mouth, and she felt his love for her there. Taking a step back, she closed her eyes and thought of the cat.

"Listen for her. She'll tell you what she wants." His voice, soft and low, seemed to settle over her. "She can feel your fear of her. Is she comforting you? Purring along your skin to let you know that she'd never hurt you?"

She felt her then; the softness of her fur as it seemed to stroke against her. When she heard Alistair's intake of breath, she opened her eyes and had to blink several times to bring him into focus.

"Christ, you're more beautiful than you were this morning." She moved to him and stumbled a little. "Careful, love. You'll need to get used to walking on four feet rather than two."

Looking down at her body, she saw the cat and knew it was her. She looked up at him, wondering for a moment how to talk to him. He moved his hand along her head, and she purred. The cat moved along his leg and rubbed against him.

"She's marking you." He laughed. *"I neve…we are two separate people, aren't we?"*

"Yes. And I wish you could see you like I do." He reached into his pocket. "Stand against the deck with your paws up on it. I want to show you what you look like."

She did as he said and heard the shutter open and close, and the small sound the phone made when he took several pictures. Ally looked out to the forest that seemed to be behind all the Golden men's homes and saw things she knew she'd never see as a human. A deer paused at the edge of the tree line. An owl was sitting on a branch several feet from the ground and watching for prey. She looked back at him as she pulled off his shirt.

"I want to run." He told her to wait. *"I can't. Please, I have to run now."* She leapt over the deck and landed on her front paws just as her back ones came down softly behind her. The deer that had been so still took off and she wanted to chase it. Taking off, she bounded over the backyard, eating up the distance in seconds. When Alistair shifted, she felt it. Her

cat seemed to know the exact moment that he was coming for her and took off more quickly.

~~~

Alistair wanted her to stay with him, but he knew she was having too much fun. He watched her and the area around them to make sure that no one came near his mate. When she tired of chasing the deer and simply played in the forest like a small child, he wished several times that he'd stayed human just to take pictures of her. She was so beautiful that every time she ran near him, he felt his heart skip several beats.

When she finally came toward him and lay down next to him, he leaned over and licked her. His cat needed this as much as she had. When she looked up at him, he could see Ally there in the cat's eyes, and fell in love with them both.

"What makes me a cat?" He was startled out of his musing when she spoke. *"I mean, I get that it's a chemical thing, I guess, but what happened when my cat came out? What happened to me?"*

"You're still there, but now there are more of you. You can reason like a human, think and speak like one to others like us, but the cat is more powerful, and she can do a little more than you." He watched as an owl swooped down and took a mouse for his dinner. *"Is that what you mean?"*

"So my cat, she's a part of me, but not really? Which of us is dominant? I mean, can I make her do things and she me?"

He thought about that before answering her. *"You're her, but you're also Ally. But can you dominate her? I suppose, but when you're in danger or afraid, she'll make her presence known to you. Especially when you're in danger. You'll feel her run along your skin because she knows that she can help you where you might not be able to handle something. Also, and this is important, when you're hurt she can heal you, and when she's hurt you can heal her by shifting. It takes a great deal of strength out of you to do it, but it may save your life."*

He felt someone in the yard seconds before she did. When she started to stand, he told her to lie close to the ground and wait for him. She did what he said, probably sensing the seriousness of it. He moved along his belly, waiting for someone to show himself, when he smelled who was there. Telling Ally to be still, he moved forward and leapt on the back of the large wolf there.

Alistair rolled him over onto his back and held his jaws at his throat. The wolf, not anyone he knew, didn't move. He felt his brother, Brock, touch his mind and started to snarl at him.

"You want to let my man go? He said he's afraid you're going to snap his neck if he tries to shift to tell you who he is." There was laughter in Brock's voice, but Alistair wasn't amused.

"I should kill his fucking ass for scaring Ally. What the hell is he doing so close to the house anyway?" Alistair let him go, but growled low when he started to stand. He waited for Brock to get back to him.

"He said that you and Ally had been playing in the woods and he didn't hear anything for the past hour. He was checking to make sure that no one had come at you from the other side. I think he's relieved that the two of you weren't having sex. I think he'd have preferred a mass murderer over that."

"Tell him to get the fuck away from here before I have to kick his ass." Brock said he would, and the wolf took off running in the opposite direction. Alistair told Ally what the man was doing.

Alistair nipped at her shoulder as she moved along his body. The excitement had gotten his juices running hot, and now he wanted an outlet for it; taking Ally out here in the forest was just the thing. He bit her hard again and watched her still.

"Remember when I first met you I told you not to run? That I would chase you down?" She said that she did. He nipped at her again before looking her in the eye. *"Run."*

Several seconds passed before she took off. Her arousal, the sweet smell of it, still lingered after she was gone. Taking as much of her scent into his mouth and nose as he could, he took off after her. He knew that as soon as he found her his cat was going to fuck her until he was satisfied.

He let her get just far enough ahead of him before he decided he'd had enough. But bringing her down wasn't as easy as he'd thought. She fought him, and fought him hard, before he could get her beneath him and hold her down. She turned to snarl at him, and he growled.

"Christ, taking you like this is something I've dreamed about my whole life." He bit into her shoulder when she tried to get away. *"Be still or I'll hurt you."*

"She wants him. She hurts so badly because she wants him to take her." He growled again and nearly came on her when her ass came up to meet him. Holding her down with his massive jaws, he slammed his cock into her.

Her scream made him hope the wolf didn't come back, but then she moved beneath him, and he could only think of how good she felt, how tightly she held him within her. Pressing her shoulders down to the ground, he fucked her hard and quick. Each time his cock moved deeper into her, she moved back against him. When his balls tightened to his body, he bit harder into her and felt her blood fill his mouth. Marking her this way was what his cat wanted, and he tore deeply into her flesh. Her scream again made him realize that she was hurt, but his cat needed everyone to know that she was his. When she cried out, both the woman and the cat, Alistair felt his cat come, his cock filling her with his seed as he continued to hold her down. As soon as he dropped onto her, he knew she needed more.

Lifting from her body, he commanded her to shift. He watched, mesmerized, as her body went from sleek cat to beautiful woman in seconds. She rolled to her back, and he licked her pussy before standing and shifting.

There was no foreplay this time. Need coiled in his body so tightly that he knew the second he entered her he was going to come again. He wanted that, wanted it more than his next breath, but he wanted her pleasure, as well. Dropping between her legs, he lifted her up so that only her shoulders touched the ground and ate her.

She tasted of him and her, their cats. Fucking her hard with his tongue, he drank deeply from her with every curl of his tongue. Settling her to the ground, he never lifted his head or stopped tasting her, knowing that she was enjoying this as much as he was. When her legs wrapped around him, he opened her nether lips with his fingers and continued his assault on her until she was begging him to fuck her. Moving up her body to fill her, he bit hard at her breast, and she cried out again.

"Now, Alistair. I can't wait much longer. Fuck me now." He slammed his cock into her, and her scream rent the air. Her nails dug deeply into his ass as she pulled him into her. Each thrust was harder than the next as she screamed over and over as she came. When she pulled him down and licked his shoulder, he felt his cock ready. Then her teeth sank into him, and he held her to him as he roared out his release.

"More," she begged him as she sealed the wound. "I need more." His body, nearly spent, seemed to rally, and when she cried out again, he joined her in a second, mind-numbing climax. Dropping on her, exhausted, he hoped that someone would find their bodies and bury them like this, because he knew he was a dead man.

The forest around them had been quiet as he lay atop of her. When he rolled to his back, taking her with him, he realized that they'd been out there long enough that a buck and his mate had wandered close to them, so close that when he rolled over he could almost touch them. As they bounded away, he lay there thinking about his own mate.

"Will it always be like this?" He grinned at her question. "Because I'm pretty sure I won't survive it if it is. That was tremendous, but very…wow."

He laughed, thinking she had it right. "We need to get up and get going soon. I can smell the rain coming." She lifted her head slightly and lay back down, telling him he was nuts.

"It'll be raining within the hour." She stretched out over him, and he felt his body stir. Telling it to behave, he hoped it would listen. He didn't really relish having to explain how he'd broken his dick because he couldn't get enough of his mate. The first fat rain drop hit him on the nose.

She lifted her head and looked down at him as the skies seemed to open up. When she jumped up with him, he laughed when she said she didn't have shoes to put on. Lifting her to his shoulder, he ran to the house and onto the deck just as lightning streaked across the sky. Standing naked under the covering on the deck, they watched the sky for several minutes before she shivered.

He took her to the hot tub, lifted the lid, and helped her into the hot water. She moaned the entire time her body was sliding into it, and he laughed when she squeaked as the jets were turned on. He then went to the refrigerator near the tub and pulled out a bottle of wine, two of the glasses that were in the freezer, and finally joined her.

"Next time we use this, I'll make sure there are snacks out here for us." He poured her some of the wine and sat back to watch her. "I love you."

"I love you, too." He had gone to his clothes that they'd taken off under the cover of the deck when he'd gotten the wine. He pulled her to him when she set her glass down. "This is really nice. I've never been in a hot tub before."

"We'll use it more in the winter than in the summer, but after what we just did, I thought we might be less sore if we used it now." He lifted her left hand to his mouth and kissed it. "Will you marry me, Ally?"

Her eyes sparkled under the twinkle lights of the canopy over the tub, so he wasn't sure if she was crying or happy. When she wrapped her arms around his neck, he nearly dropped the ring. He laughed when she screamed.

"I'm guessing that's a yes?" She kissed his entire face and then grabbed him and kissed him fully on the mouth before she lifted her head.

"Yes. Yes. Yes, I'll marry you."

Alistair didn't think that anything in the world could make him any happier than he was at that moment. He slipped on the ring, then held her close to him. He wondered how long they'd have to wait before she'd let him make it legal.

"Do you think you can talk a judge into marrying us soon?" she said, looking up at him. "I'd really like to be your wife for the rest of my life. And the sooner the better."

Yes, Alistair thought, he was one happy man.

CHAPTER 11

It took him the better part of the day to get to the house. And by the time he got there, Lance couldn't believe how sore he was. Not only his feet but his entire body felt as if he'd been run over by a couple of trucks and then left for dead. Glad now that he'd found a blanket and had purchased a backpack to put his crap in, he dropped it on the ground and dropped beside it.

He'd left the phone at the hotel. He'd not had the money to waste on it anyway, and had decided that sooner or later someone would find out where he was and come for him. Leaving behind his extra clothes hadn't even been as difficult as he'd thought it would have been. He knew that the chances of him getting to wear them again were slim to none. He knew as surely as he was sitting there that this was his last stand.

Finding Alistair's house had been a little more difficult than the map in the phone book had led him to believe. He knew it was far but not like this. And there were streets along the way that weren't on the map, and he'd gotten turned around several times before he realized it. As soon as he figured out the main street that ran in front of the house, he'd stuck to it like glue until he started to see addresses that matched the one in the phone book. Lance only hoped that now that he was here that the phone book was up to date.

Pulling out a bottle of water and a long stick of meat he'd picked up at Wal-Mart, he ate it like it was the best steak he'd ever eaten. He almost ate a second one but didn't know how long he was going to have to be here before he could leave to go back to the mammoth store.

He'd been surprised at how much stuff was in the place. Having never shopped at Wal-Mart before in his life, he'd thought it was just a place for people without much or any money. They had had brand names that he'd heard of, and so much in the way of food that he wondered if his mother had ever been in one. Then he'd laughed.

Not her. She would more than likely turn her nose up at what he'd called his dinner if he were to show it to her. She'd have him shower several times, and would have him burn his clothes as well. He and his mother were better than most people they knew, and not a one of them would have believed that he had lowered himself to shop there.

Settling against the tree, he closed his eyes and decided that napping for a bit might be the best thing. But his mind wouldn't shut off, and all he could think about was the mess that Allyson had gotten them into. Had she just done what he'd told her to things would be just fine. He might even have found himself a wife to settle down with for good in her. But she'd run, and now he was going to prison for the rest of his life if nothing else. She'd caused all this.

Lance knew that blaming her was stupid. She'd not gotten him into the financial mess they were in. That had started long before his father had put a bullet in his own head. But he needed someone to blame. And she was there.

Rolling to his side, he wondered if anyone would miss him. He wondered, too, if he'd ever be discussed around dinner tables as a great lawyer. He could have been, he supposed, but the love of money had been a bigger prize to him. And a great deal more fun than defending idiots that were more times than not guilty of whatever mess he'd been trying to save them from.

He wondered if he should leave the country, a question many of his clients had asked at the initial consultation. Lately he'd told them to stay so he could milk the firm rather than telling them to run when they had no chance at all of coming out on top.

Feeling his body relax enough that he thought he could sleep, he let himself slide away. He would need his strength to deal with Ally and her new boyfriend. He'd rather not have to deal with Alistair knowing that the man was in better shape than he'd ever be, but the man also had that powerful brother. Not that Alistair was a small man, but the other man, Brock, he remembered his name to be, just seemed to be born to intimidate. Lance shivered when he thought of the men, and wondered if the rumors he'd heard all through college were true, that there were half a dozen of the Golden men and one was about as relentless as the other, and as mean as they came when it came to family.

He heard a car and startled awake, not realizing that he'd been asleep at all. When they paused nearby, Lance figured they were sitting at the end of the drive and waiting. He had no idea if they were coming or going and didn't want to be caught here so close to his goal. When the sound drifted away, he lifted his head and looked around.

It was a little darker than when he'd gotten here. Not complete black out but dark enough. He thought about taking out his flashlight but thought he'd wait for a little while longer. He wasn't sure how long the cheap batteries he'd purchased would last, and he didn't have but the one set of them. He just sat there, finished off his water, and devoured another beef stick. Then he went out to a tree deep in the woods and pissed on it, then to another one to mark his territory. He had no idea why he'd done it, and felt foolish when he sat back at his little home.

Lance decided that when it was fully dark he'd go in and see what he could do about killing Allyson. He was under no delusions that he was only going to hurt her, or even to take her home again. He was going to kill her with his bare hands as soon as he got her.

When the car returned, he'd been so startled that he simply let the light flash over him without moving to hide. Several cars had passed him in the time he'd been waiting, and when this one turned in the drive and stopped at the gates, he'd nearly missed his opportunity to enter. Scrambling up, he ran to the opening and realized he'd forgotten his backpack and rushed back for it. The doors were closing just as he slipped past them and onto the grounds. Smiling, he thought this was going to be easier than he'd ever dreamed it would be.

~~~

Ryland handed him the next file as they went through everything that had been brought by the Cooks, and there was a great deal of it. There were pictures of Isaac on a boat with other women, and one of him coming out of shops with bags of purchases. There was even one of him when he'd married Ally. Even back then, Alistair thought she looked unhappy.

"According to the date on this picture, this was taken three days after he married Ally. He didn't wait long before he began cheating on her, did he?" Alistair took the picture of him on the boat and looked at the woman. He handed it to Ally.

"This is another woman that worked at the firm. I'm not sure if I ever actually met her, but she'd always be at the same parties that we were required to attend. He would disappear for hours on end and leave me there while he was probably beating on someone else for a change." She laid the picture down and stood up.

Alistair was afraid she was going to go and bake something again. He hoped she didn't. He'd put on a little weight since she'd moved in, and he knew that the others had, too. Ryland eyed the cookies she'd brought them earlier.

"I think I'm going to watch some television. I can't look at this anymore." Both of them nodded as she left the room.

"She's taking this better than I thought she would." Alistair nodded at his brother's statement. "I tried to get Bronwyn to come with me, but she said she wasn't feeling good and lay down. Mom is supposed to call if she needs me."

Bronwyn was getting more and more tired lately, and bigger, too. He knew that pregnant women got large when they were having a baby, but he worried that she was going to hurt herself carrying around the extra weight. He'd never say anything to her, but he was frightened for her.

"I heard from the police about the shooting at the courthouse. They said that the man who shot all those people had been sentenced to death row about five years ago. He'd gotten out when a clerk at the county office had misread his number and released him instead of a man with nearly the same number." Alistair handed Ryland a file that had nothing to do with the ones they were working on. "One of the judges he killed was the one that had sent him up. He also managed to kill his prosecutor, as well. I'm sure the clerk is looking for another job about now."

"Christ," Ryland said as he gave in and took two of the cookies off the plate. "Take them suckers out of here. I love your mate to death, but she's going to have us all as fat as we can get before much longer."

Laughing, he set the cookies on the table behind him. It wasn't far, but it was far enough that he'd have to make an effort to get to them. He looked at Ryland when he cleared his throat.

"Bronwyn said to tell you to keep her close over the next few days. She didn't say why, but she said that she thought that Isaac was closer than we thought." Alistair nodded. "She also said that she could be wrong, that her hormones are all over the place lately, and she can't seem to get a grip on them."

"But you think she's right." It wasn't really a question, but Ryland nodded anyway. "We have the wedding tomorrow. Then I have a court appearance after noon. Jed said he'd go with me to keep an eye on her until it's over. I think he's a little in love with her."

"We all are. She's an amazing woman." Ryland laughed. "Putting up with you is enough reason for us to put her up on a pedestal, but we do feel sorry for you about that, too."

They looked over a few more files until Jed came in with two bottles of beer and a plate of carrot and celery sticks. Both men looked at it, then up at the cook.

"You said yourself that you needed to eat better. I'm helping. Besides, you didn't hear this from me, but she's been baking again. I think she's hoping to have a nice little wedding cake ready for tomorrow evening for everyone." They looked at the kitchen. "She's not cooking now, but had been until a bit ago. She's watching something on the television in there with me. I think she's more scared than she's letting on."

Alistair reached for her and could feel the tension in her body. She was afraid, not for herself but for all of them. He told Ryland that he needed a break, and his brother said he needed to get home anyway. The information they had now was enough to bury the man, and getting any more was just overkill.

After Ryland left, Alistair went into the kitchen to find her helping Jed with dinner. They were having pork chops and au gratin potatoes, green beans, and peach cobbler for dessert. The two of them were laughing about something she was telling Jed about that she'd seen on television.

"And then he turned around, and there his wife was. Who in the world would say something like that about his wife and not expect her to find out?" She grinned at him when she saw him. "I was just coming to get you. Jed has agreed to eat with us tonight."

He glanced at the other man to see him shaking his head. Jed had cooked for him for nearly ten years, and he'd never seen the man look so panic-stricken. Laughing to himself, Alistair said he thought it was an excellent idea and helped put the things on the table. He figured sooner or later he'd pay for this, but she seemed to so happy to have him dining with them that he couldn't let the man off the hook.

It was nearing midnight when they went up to bed. Jed said he'd come in early tomorrow to get them out the door on time. Everyone was going to meet them at the courthouse. Then Alistair was headed over to another part of the building for a trial that he was hoping to get an extension on. He was sure he could, but the way things had been going lately, he thought maybe it wouldn't happen that way.

Ally was in the tub when he came into the bedroom. He watched her as she shaved her legs, the razor sliding down her leg covered in bubbles. She grinned up at him when she finished the erotic stroke.

"You're not coming in here tonight. Tomorrow is our wedding, and I want it to be special." He sat down on the toilet and took her foot into his hands. "I mean it, Alistair. If I have to go down the hall to sleep, you are going to behave yourself."

"Oh, and what makes you think I would let you? Besides, I can make tonight and tomorrow night special for you." He grinned at her when she jerked her foot from him. "Oh baby, you're killing me here. I just want to show you how much I love you."

"Go away." He stood up and started out of the room, but stopped suddenly and pulled her up for a long, hard kiss.

"I want you to remember that when you're sleeping in our bed alone." She turned in the tub as he started out.

"You're not sleeping with me?" He shook his head. "Why not? I thought we could just hold each other tonight."

"No. If I get into that bed with you, I'm going to hold you, all right! Beneath me while I fill you with my cock. Then maybe after you come several times, I'll be able to simply hold you."

He watched her face as she digested what he'd said. He wanted her, but had planned to sleep in one of the spare bedrooms anyway. He moved out of the room and picked up his case that he'd packed earlier. She called out for him before he left, and he came back to her, holding tightly on the case in the event she was standing there naked when he went back.

"You're not mad at me, are you?" He shook his head at her question. "I guess it's sort of stupid to think that after sleeping together all this time, one night would make much of a difference."

"It will and it does. I love you very much, and even though we're not going to have this grand wedding, there isn't any reason why we can't have a spectacular wedding night." He showed her the case. "I had already planned to sleep alone, thinking about all the things I plan to do to you as soon as you're my wife."

"I don't want a large wedding. I want what we're having. I don't…the first wedding was a major disaster, and I don't need a reminder of what a fool I'd been." She turned back in the tub and started on the other leg. "And being your wife will give me more than I've ever wanted. Plus, I'll have your name and not his. After tomorrow, everything about him will be erased from my memory."

Alistair left her to her bath and moved down the hall. He hoped that tomorrow would give her more and better memories, because he knew that until he was out of their life completely, Lance Isaac was going to be nothing they'd be able to forget.

Knowing he wasn't going to be able to sleep, he pulled the file on the hearing for the next day. After reading over the same page three times, he tossed it on the desk. He got up, opened the door to the balcony, and stepped out onto the small deck there.

The night was quiet, and it took him several seconds of listening to realize that it was too quiet. He was reaching for Brock to see if he had someone on the property when he saw a wolf run across the yard. The stupid thing was chasing something…he thought it was a deer, maybe. If he brought it down and Ally found out about it she'd probably have him murdered.

Then the deer came running back the other way. He laughed when the wolf took off in the opposite direction. Stupid mutts didn't have a clue how to hunt and to be quiet when they did. Alistair closed the doors and slipped off his clothes.

Tomorrow he was going to be married. He had heard that some tigers, even other species, sometimes married for the companionship, and he wondered what they did with their wives if their mate showed up later. He had already decided that he'd wait for his mate even if it took nearly all his life to find her. He'd been a little jealous of Ryland when he'd found his mate, and now he knew just how his brother had felt.

Rolling to his back, he smiled. She was going to have a brick when she found out what he'd done about their honeymoon. In two weeks, they were going to Paris and a few other countries for an entire month. And when they returned, he was going to take her away for another month just for the hell of it. Alistair closed his eyes. He was going to be married in the morning, and he couldn't have been any happier.

CHAPTER 12

She waited in the bathroom, hoping that she didn't have to throw up again. Ally glanced over at Bronwyn and grinned. The woman looked ready to pop, and she still had seven weeks to go. When Bronwyn noticed she was looking at her, she glared.

"I could so make you slip and fall on your ass if you laugh at me." She would, too, and Ally knew it. "I'm so fucking miserable that I can't move without wanting to take a nap. It's this weather. Why is it so hot in April?"

It was hot. It had been nearly ninety yesterday and was supposed to top that today. She handed her the bottle of water that Brock had given her when she'd rushed past him.

"Just a few days ago it was in the forties, and now it's in the hundreds. Do you think it would have been more tolerable had it built up slowly and not frozen us one day and boiled us the next?" Bronwyn nodded and rubbed the bottle on her head. "I suppose it'd be too much to ask to turn on the air."

Bronwyn looked at her and smiled. She wasn't sure she'd ever seen that smile before, and hoped whatever she was thinking wasn't directed at her. She closed her eyes for a second and then looked at her and stood up.

"It'll be cool in here soon. I should have thought of that earlier." She didn't ask her what she'd done. Not knowing, she thought, would keep her innocent. She walked by one of the maintenance men who were standing in front of a thermostat. Ally had a feeling people were going to need coats in about an hour.

The judge's office where the wedding was going to take place was closed. Ally glanced at her watch and realized she still had ten minutes to go. She looked up at Ryland when he came out of the office and closed the door behind him.

"You about ready?" She nodded at him. He'd told her yesterday, when she'd ask him to give her away—a formality that wasn't really necessary in a court house—that he'd be honored. He told her he'd even put on a tie. Bronwyn told her that was a big deal, because he'd not even wanted to wear one at his own wedding. He handed her a spray of white and yellow roses and told her they were from Alistair.

She felt the tears fill her eyes and looked at Bronwyn. These people had come to mean so much to her that she didn't know what she'd do if anything happened to them. When Bronwyn hugged her, she felt like she finally had a family...more so than she'd had with even her own mother. The others came running down the hall just as she was about to go in.

"Wait. I have something for you." Keith handed her another spray of roses; these were pink. "We wanted you to have a shit ton of flowers."

Jules handed her bright red ones, and Neal handed her the most delicate shade of blue she'd ever seen. Brock was inside with his brother, but Ryland handed her a beautiful single rose that had been dyed a light green. He told her it was from Brock.

"And so you know, I bought you a rose bush." She laughed. "I wanted you to remember me every time it bloomed."

She laughed when Keith called his brother a sap. And when someone knocked on the other side of the judge's door she looked at them all. "I've never been so...I love you all very much. I can't tell you what it means to me to have you all here."

None of them spoke as Brock opened the door and told them they were ready. When she walked into the chambers, her breath caught. There stood Alistair in his suit, his brother Brock to his left, and his mom standing right beside them. And the room was filled with every kind of flower known to man.

"Oh my." She reached out and put her hand on Ryland's arm, suddenly overwhelmed with it all, with them all. When Alistair came forward and took her hands she looked up at him and smiled.

"I love you." She nodded, sure that if she tried to speak she'd blubber and sob. "You're going to be my wife for all time, and I plan to make you look like you do now, happy and in love, for the rest of my life."

He pulled her forward with Ryland on her other side. As soon as they were standing before the judge, the music started playing softly. Judge Sanders smiled at her.

"You are a very lovely woman. All Alistair's been talking about all morning is how he had the most beautiful wife in the world." She flushed and looked at Alistair.

The ceremony went off with almost nothing going wrong. The only thing that happened was when Brock's cell phone went off and everyone glared at him. He flushed a bright red and turned it off.

Alistair slipped the ring on her finger with a shaky breath. He told her he loved her, and then kissed her when he'd done it. The judge cleared his throat.

"We've not gotten to that part yet, boy. Hold your horses." Everyone laughed. "Okay, then. We'll start over if you make me lose my place again."

The rest went smoothly, and before Alistair kissed her at the right time, he turned to the judge and asked for permission. The man blushed and told him to behave.

There was a light brunch served in a closed office that Jed had prepared for them. The wedding cake that she'd made was sitting in the middle of it all. She and Alistair cut it, and with lots of cell phone cameras going off, he smashed in it her face, and she did the same to him, only she didn't get to rub it in his hair like she wanted to because he had to go to court. A lot of people came by to wish them well. Then, all too soon, Alistair told her he had to leave.

"I'm hoping to be finished in a couple of hours…that is, if I can't get a continuance. But seeing how the judge for that appearance knows we just got married, I'm hoping he'll let it go until tomorrow. I want to take you to the nearest empty office I can find and take you hard against the wall." She shivered at the thought of him doing just that. His low growl made her cat race along her skin.

"Stop that." She looked up at him and saw that his cat was there, as well. "We're going to make a scene if we keep this up."

"Christ, I hope so." He pulled her into his arms and kissed her. She could feel his cock harden against her and she moaned. When he pulled away she wasn't sure if she could stand by herself.

"You'd better be naked and in bed when I get there. I swear to you if you're not then you're going to have to

replace whatever you had on, because it won't survive me."
She shivered again and felt her pussy heat. "I can smell you.
Christ."

He took a step back and then another. She grinned at him
when he tugged his jacket down over his erection. When he
glared, she laughed out loud. With a quick kiss to her nose, he
left her standing in the empty hall. She went back to the
chambers and told Jed she was ready any time he was.

They were going to go and pick up a few things, then
they were going to hit the kitchen store. She hadn't been in
one since before she married Lance, and was as excited as Jed
appeared to be. It was within walking distance of the
courthouse, but they had decided that if they purchased
anything that they'd have to lug it back, and this would be
easier. Besides, she had plans to purchase a great deal.

The kitchen at their house was beautiful, but it was
outdated in the way of appliances. There was a toaster that
had to be talked sweetly to before it would work, a tea maker
that had a crack in the pitcher, as well, as it leaked out the
back. Also, there was no stand mixer, and nothing in the way
of a food processor, all things that she and Jed could use on a
daily basis. She thought about the herbs that he and she had
started just last week that were just starting to sprout.

"I think we should look at these as well." She moved over
to where he was standing in front of all sorts of gadgets.
Before she could say anything he spoke low to her. "Someone
is following us."

She stilled, and when he handed her a shiny spatula, she
used it to look behind her. She didn't know the man. She
handed it back to Jed and then started to turn but "accidently"
knocked a box off the shelf beside her, and looked at the man
as she bent over.

"I don't know him." Jed nodded and told her to continue shopping. He handed her several more things and told her to put them in her basket. She had no idea what he was giving her, because she was worried about the man behind him. When Jed relaxed, she did as well.

"He left. Maybe I was just being paranoid." She nodded but didn't think so, and she didn't think he did, either. "Come on. Let's get that coffee maker over there, and I want to see about getting a waffle maker. The one we have now is about three hundred years old and sticks really bad."

They took another hour to get all they wanted, and the owner of the shop helped them carry it out to their car. She was glad now that Jed had brought the large SUV, because she was sure that the little car he owned wouldn't have cut it. Her phone was ringing while Jed closed the back of the car up. She was happy to see it was from Alistair.

"I'm going to be here most of the day. I'm sorry. The man was bitching about his lack of accommodations in his cell of all things, and now he wants things finished today. Since everything is pretty much settled except for what he owes, we're going to finish this. The good news is I have the next three days off, then the weekend." She leaned against the car, disappointed.

"I'm sorry, too. But you might want to stay working. I just spent a small national debt for the kitchen, and we've not even looked at refrigerators or stoves yet." He laughed. "I wish you could be with us."

"You and Jed do most of the cooking, and I'd be out of place. And I can be surprised when you bring it all home for us." He spoke to someone, and she waited. "I have to go, love. I can't wait to get home to you. I'm going to taste every part of you, then do it again before I come deep inside of you."

Hanging up, she stayed leaning against the car for several seconds until Jed stepped in front of her. He was grinning, and she thought he could tell what she and Alistair had been talking about.

"Are all men like him?" He shrugged. "I love him dearly, but I tell you, sometimes I just want to smack him silly."

"I'm sure he knows that, too." He opened the door for her. "Did you tell him that we've spent all his money?"

"Yes, and he didn't care. I think I'm going to buy the most expensive refrigerator they have just for spite." Jed laughed at her and went around to his side of the car. She wasn't sure, but she thought he said Alistair wouldn't care. She thought he was right. Damned man.

The appliance store was a dream come true. She and Jed spent an hour in the stove area alone. They ended up with a range with a convection oven as well as a regular oven, and bought a microwave as well to match the stainless steel. The refrigerators were just as nice, but other than the ice maker on the front, she'd not had much to contribute for that decision. Jed, however, seemed to know just what he wanted, and the man helping them was making his money from him. She smiled when he finally got what he needed.

"We'll have it delivered tomorrow morning and have the others taken away at no charge, if you'd like." She nodded, not knowing what, if anything, Alistair would want to do with them. And, as they were walking back out to the parking garage with their few purchases, she realized she'd forgotten her sunglasses.

"I'll go and get them and you can meet me here with the car." Jed looked around like he wasn't sure, and she told him she'd be fine. "I swear I know where they are. I'll just go get them and come right back out. Five minutes."

"All right, but if you're one second longer, I'm coming for you. And I won't be happy." She nodded and hurried back inside. They were just where she'd left them. She turned and left immediately after grabbing them. When the doors to the elevator opened, she expected to see Jed and the car right in front of her. She didn't see anything.

She started toward where the car had been parked, and was just walking by a pylon when someone stepped out in front of her. She felt fear race along her skin when she recognized the man from the kitchen shop.

"You're not an easy woman to find." She started to take a step back and hit something hard. A gun suddenly appeared in his hand. "I wouldn't do that if I were you. I'm going to kill you, but I'd rather do it where we're less likely to be heard. Your buddy made enough noise."

She looked back where the car was. "Did you kill him? Please, I don't know why you're doing this, but don't hurt Jed. He's just a good man."

He stared at her for several seconds, and she had a feeling that he was shocked about something. "You really don't know, do you? You have no idea why she wants you dead."

"I don't…I know that my ex-husband wants me to come back with him, but not a woman. Does this have anything to do with the mall shooting? Is it the same woman?"

He hit her. She felt blood erupt from her mouth and nose immediately. She cringed when he stepped closer to her.

"That wasn't my fault. I told him to be careful and not to kill anyone but you, but he had to make a name for himself." He hit her again, this time making her dizzy. "You'll not say another word about that, or so help me I'll make you suffer in ways you never did with that fucking bitch of a mother-in-law."

"Mrs. Isaac hired you?" She tried to think why. Then he started talking again and jerked her toward him. "She doesn't hate me that much, does she?"

The man was dragging her away from the car she and Jed had come in, and she was glad. If Jed was alive, he'd not be shot by this man. She tripped twice and he slammed her against another pylon.

He hit her again just as she felt something touch her mind. It was Alistair. She was losing her hold on staying conscious, and screamed at him through their link. *"He's going to kill me. It's Lance's mom who hired the man to kill me in both places. We're in the parking garage at the appliance store on Tenth, and I think Jed is dead. You have to come and save him, if you can."*

Something moved. She saw it just as her vision blurred, and wondered how in the world Alistair had gotten to her so quickly. Then the screams. She wasn't sure if it was her or not, because her body became too heavy for her, and she slipped away.

~~~

Alistair tore from the room and never looked back. He reached for his brothers and told them to get to her. As soon as he was in the parking garage, he reached for her again and felt nothing. Terror like nothing he'd ever felt in his life shrouded over him like a blanket. He had to take several deep breaths before he could answer Brock.

"She said that it was Isaac's mother who hired the hit man. She said Jed was hurt and to come and save him for her." He took another breath. *"I can't think. I have no idea where I'm at."*

"I'm driving by the courthouse now, and I'll pick you up. Be out front. Can you do that?" He told him that he could.

"We're going to get to her, Alistair. She's strong and smart. She'll be fine."

What seemed an eternity later, Brock pulled up in front up the courthouse. He got in the passenger's seat. Keith was in the back with Jules. Each man looked as scared as he felt.

"They were at the appliance store on Tenth Street. I don't know if I ever knew the name of it." Brock nodded, taking a corner a little too sharply as Alistair realized he was babbling. "I have to find her. All I'm getting is emptiness."

They pulled up behind the cruiser that was already there. An ambulance pulled up behind them, and Brock was told he had to move. When he handed the keys over to Jules, Brock and Keith followed him into the fray. They were stopped only once, and after that everyone gave them a wide berth. Alistair wasn't sure what Brock had said to the cops, but he was glad now that he'd stopped to pick him up. The man in front of them was a friend of the family, Shaller James, and he was a wolf. He held him back before the yellow tape.

"You can't go in there. Not yet, at any rate. Do you know the victim?" His world seemed to pinpoint for a second, and the next thing he knew, he was sitting on the floor with his head between his legs. "I'm sorry, Alistair. I should have said that better. There's a human male there with a female cat. I heard you recently took a mate. Tell me what she looks like."

He couldn't speak, but Brock did. He looked up to see Shaller nodding. "It's her. She's out and beaten up pretty badly, but is going to be fine, I think. The man? He's been mauled to death. But she didn't do it."

"What do you mean she...who else was here?" Shaller nodded to just behind him, and he saw Jed there. Or at least he thought it was Jed. The cat staring back at him looked like he'd taken a bath in blood, and he sat there shivering.

"No one but the two of you, and I know he's there. I assume you know him, as well?" Alistair nodded. "He can go home, but he…I'm not at all sure what happened here, but she's been beat to shit, and I've a dead man here that has…Christ, he tore him up. I'll be finding pieces of him for months."

"He saved her." Shaller told him it looked that way. "I can't leave him here. The first human who sees him will kill him."

"Get him home with you, please. I'm going to have your mate taken to the clinic that you run. It's not closer, but I think once she wakes she'll be fine." Shaller leaned down and spoke to him softly. "I need a story, Alistair. People are going to panic if they hear a cat was involved."

"I'll take care of it. What are you saying now?" He told him unknown assailant. "I'll see what I can do. I'll talk to you after I get Ally taken care of. When can I see her?"

A gurney slipped up beside them, and he stood. He looked down at her face and felt rage at what she looked like. He looked at Brock.

"Get Jed out of here and I'll meet you at the clinic. He'll… he said he'd never shift again, but he did when she needed him."

"I'll get him out. You make sure you contact me when you hear anything. After I get him home, I'll come back." He nodded and got into the ambulance with Ally. Her hand was cool but not cold. He held it all the way to the clinic, thinking about what could have happened. But he knew one thing for sure. Jed had saved his mate by doing something he'd sworn he'd never do again. Shifting for his mate had more than likely saved her life, and Alistair knew that he would owe the man for the rest of his life and then some.

CHAPTER 13

Ally felt as if she was rising from a deep dive. She couldn't seem to get enough air in her lungs. When she opened her eyes, she wasn't sure what she expected to see, but the stranger standing over her wasn't it. Her fist connected with his jaw, and he fell away from her.

She tried to sit up, but she hurt. When she realized she could hear someone laughing, she looked to her right, and there sat her family. She started crying the moment she saw Alistair.

"Jed. You have to tell me where Jed is. That man said he'd killed him, but he's not...what's so funny?" She glared at Alistair as the man she'd slugged stood up. He started to back away from her when she tried to sit up again.

"This is your doctor and my friend, Hansel Lipscomb. He was checking your vitals when you hit him." She looked at the man again. "He said he thought you'd be out for a few more hours."

"And I am willing to admit I was wrong." Hansel laughed as he reached for her hand. "I need to record these. Could you try and refrain from knocking me on my ass for another minute?"

"You startled me. Last thing I remembered is some man…." She looked at the two men. "He's dead, isn't he? You killed him."

"I didn't kill anyone, love, but if you mean the man who hit you, then yes, he's dead. He's been hurt when a drug deal went the wrong way and he ended up being dragged behind a car through the parking lot." She looked at him oddly and decided that whatever was going on he'd better explain later. "As for Jed? He's on his way in. He had to…he needed to get cleaned up before he could come back with Keith."

"But that man—" His head shook very quickly, and she closed her mouth. She was trying to figure it out when Jed came in the door just as the doctor was going out. She leapt from the bed to hold him. Not even the growls from Alistair could make her let him go.

"You're all right then?" She ran her hands over his shoulders and arms before he captured them and held them in his one hand. She looked up at him. "I thought he'd killed you. He said he had."

"I'm fine. Better than fine, and will live a great deal longer, love, if you would please stop marking me." He took a step back, and she felt the tears well in her eyes. Sometimes this cat thing was a pain in the ass. She looked at Alistair.

"He was hurt. I needed to make sure he was all right. I didn't want to cause a huge fight." He pulled her into his arms, and she sobbed against his chest while he held her. She heard the door open and close, and figured everyone had left the big baby to cry. She looked up at Alistair and saw that Jed was still in the room with them.

"What I'm going to tell you very few will ever know about. You'll never be able to tell anyone what happened today. All right?" She nodded and sat back down on the bed while Alistair started to pace as he spoke. "When you called out to me I was in the courtroom. I couldn't get to you. Not in time. I left there as soon as you blanked out from me. Tell me what you two remember."

"He hit my head a few times and I was trying to hang on." He nodded at her. "He told me that he'd been there to kill me because Lance's mother had hired him. He even admitted that the murders at the mall had been something he'd been responsible for as well. He said that it wasn't his fault. That the man who'd been sent to kill me had to go too far." She looked at Jed. "He was the man from the kitchen store, the one that left before we did."

"Yes. He followed us, I guess, and when you went into the store to get your sunglasses, he jumped me. I don't know what he hit me with, but he knocked me out pretty easily. I think if he had hit a human he would have killed him. But me being a super, well, he didn't hit hard enough." Jed laughed as he continued. "He made a mistake by not shooting me when he had the chance."

She shivered and looked at Alistair. "But you said it was a drug deal. And that the man had been dragged behind a car. What happened to him? If it's not the same man, we need to—"

"It was the same man that attacked you. And he is dead. The police are telling that story so we don't have to explain why he'd been mauled to death by a large tiger. Shaller didn't want to cause a panic and have idiots out hunting for animals that don't really exist." She frowned, not understanding.

"But you said you never made it to me. You didn't help me." She tried to think. "But I saw you there. You flew at him just as he was going to kill me. I saw you."

"You saw a cat, honey, but it wasn't me." She looked at him, then at Jed when he did. "Jed and you were the only two tigers in the area when the man attacked you."

It took her a few seconds for it to sink in. "You shifted." Jed nodded at her and flushed a deep red.

"I had to. I couldn't...he was bent on killing you." She nodded and took his hand in hers. "I didn't think I'd ever have reason to shift again, and when I saw him put that gun to your head, I had to do something. I...." He put his head down, and she watched as his big shoulders shook as he cried.

Looking at Alistair, he nodded. She pulled Jed into her arms. He cried as if his heart was broken, and she didn't know why. Then he lifted his head and looked at her, his eyes red, and his face tearstained.

"You saved me, Ally. All this time...I've not wanted to go on any more, not like this. My cat had...I thought he'd left me, and I was so depressed. Then you come along and bring me to life, make my cat start to stir again. But I didn't know you'd made him live." He leaned his forehead against hers. "I love you. I love you more than I ever did anyone before. I can't...I will never be able to repay you for all you've done for me."

She held him for several more minutes before he pulled away from her. He sat in the chair as Alistair told her what had happened after the man had been dealt with. Alistair told them the reason for the elaborate story.

"Jed isn't being charged with anything. That's the reason for the story. There was no way that we could explain the death, especially how he'd been...Jed made sure he'd never bother us again."

"But Mrs. Isaac? What do we do about her?" Alistair grinned, and she smiled back at him. "You have a plan."

"I do. And as far as anyone is concerned right now, you're dead."

~~~

"What do you mean, it's over? Over how?" Lance looked down the road as another car approached the phone booth where he was. "Are you saying that she's dead?"

"Yes. I heard it on the news about an hour ago." He had walked into town to get more food when he'd had the urge to call his mother if only to hear her voice. She'd said his name and told him to answer her right now. "It's all over the news. Said she was accidently killed during a drug buy gone badly. That makes it double the pay off, right?"

It did, but he still didn't believe it. He'd been sitting at the house for nearly four days, and some punk killed her in a drug buy? He leaned against the phone booth and tried to think what to do now. He could collect.

"When can you come home? I can't claim the insurance because everything is in your name." The way she'd said it made him frown. *She* couldn't collect the money? Why was she even trying?

"I have to make sure. There might be…it might be a trap." A huge one if it was, but he'd heard of them before. "Let me see what I can find out down here and I'll get back to you. I don't…I'm not even sure how to get home right now. I'm broke."

"You'll come home now. I've been waiting for this thing to pay off for months, and now that the money is ours, I want it. I've got to…did you know that the bank is auctioning off all my lovely things? Why did you let that happen to me?" She sobbed a little, and he knew he had hurt her again. He'd heard it before. "You're as bad as your father."

"Mom, I…please don't cry. I'm so sorry. I really am. But I have no money here. Nothing. I had to steal the little I have to call you." He looked at the twenty-eight cents he had left after taking a woman's purse from her grocery cart an hour before. "In a very short time they are going to disconnect us, and I'm not going to be able to call you back."

"You have to get here. I need you. You're—" The line went dead. He sat down on the sidewalk and waited. He wondered if she'd call him back, and waited for ten minutes before he picked up his purchases and started back to the house. Why he was going, he had no idea. If Allyson was dead, he had no reason to stick around.

Lance was about an hour down the road when he heard a car coming up behind him. He started to move into the dark bushes but actually didn't care. He watched it drive by him and noted that he'd had a car like it at one time. A dark Mercedes that had leather-heated seats and everything else he'd wanted. Now he had a bag of sticks of meat and bottled water, he'd not had a bath in five days, and he was pretty sure he had a horrible case of poison ivy on his dick.

"Christ, how the mighty have fallen." He moved to where he'd been staying for several days. He'd gotten onto the property once, but had nearly been eaten by a pack of giant wolves. Actually, they'd never seen him, but he'd seen them, all right, and got the fuck out as soon as he could. They were the biggest fucking things he'd ever seen.

He thought about getting back in, breaking into the house, and seeing if she really was dead. He had no way to take her, he'd realized after a couple of days of being there, and not even a gun to kill her with. He wished, as he had for weeks now, that he'd never seen or heard of Allyson or her money, and especially not anything to do with insurance scams.

Settling down, he knew that he should simply turn himself in and be done with it. But he couldn't make himself do that either. He wasn't a bad person. He had only wanted what he felt had been owed to him, and somehow he'd gotten lost along the way. He grinned when he thought of the lengths he'd gone to when he'd wanted something, and wondered why this was any different. He sat up and looked at the gate that held him out.

They would have some kind of weapon in there, right? They would have a knife or even a gun, maybe, to kill her. If nothing else he'd bet he could find something from the garage. Poison or even a rake or an axe. He could use an axe on her and it would be over with in no time.

He eyed the gate again. All he had to do was stand far enough away from the camera so that when he moved in behind a car no one would see him. He'd been watching it for days now, and knew that when someone pulled up they spoke in the microphone. Then, once granted permission, he would move in. He could do that, slip in behind a car, and into the gates to the house. She'd be dead by nightfall if she wasn't already.

He heard a car and tensed. He wasn't in place yet. Watching it slow, he knew that it was one of the ones that had been coming and going for days now, and waited until it was beyond the gate before he moved to the bushes. Someone always followed this car. He'd actually been wondering why there was so much activity at this place. He was about to find out.

He heard the car approach and waited, moving back farther into the darkness as it slowed and moved into position. He had a tempting moment when he almost opened the door and got into the vehicle, but realized that like most cars it would be locked and he'd give his position away. As soon as the gate started to slide open he moved up to the front of the car. And when it moved, he did as well.

Lance followed along the car for several yards before he lost his footing and fell. He let himself roll for several feet, knowing that whoever was driving would have been able to see him from the rearview mirrors if he simply lay there. Looking down at his leg he realized he'd cut it up pretty badly, but it was nothing he wasn't able to walk on. As he limped along the tree-lined drive, he started to feel like this was going to work.

He stopped after going around the driveway's bend. He had expected a large house, but nothing on the scale of this one. It was twice as big as his, and the surrounding property looked to be a great deal more substantial. As he moved closer he realized that not only was there the one home, but there seemed to be a second, smaller home in the back. He surmised it to be a maid's home, or the cooks.

"Christ, I should have made a friend of him in college rather than turn my nose up at him." He moved toward the large eight bay garage and slipped into one of the open bays. He could only stare at the cars that sat in the neat rows inside. And at the end of three of the bays were motorcycles; one vintage, one newer, and one that looked like it had cost as much as his last car. He was moving toward it when he heard voices and moved to roll under the closest car. He realized his mistake almost immediately. What if they got into this car?

"I tell you I saw something. I think it was someone coming in with Jed." Lance closed his eyes and waited for them to look under the car for him. "He looked like that prick that's been in all the papers. The one that they have the manhunt for."

"Lance Isaac? You don't think that guy is that stupid, do you? I mean, why would he come here of all days? Her funeral is today." The voice sounded familiar, and he realized it was Alistair. "He wouldn't have the nerve to show up today, would he?"

So she was dead. He laid his head back on the floor and wondered what to do now. He was just trying to figure out

154

how to get back out of this place and get home when Alistair spoke again.

"Let's put the donations in here. That way we won't have to worry about them getting lost when people start showing up." Lance watched where they moved to and waited. "Then tomorrow we'll come out and get it and take it to the bank. She would have liked for us to have the money donated to the Paula Cook foundation."

"Yeah, she was an awesome woman. I'm going to miss her dearly." Lance smiled. The two men walked out and he heard the door to the house open and close. Before he could get caught he went to where they'd been and looked through the cabinet for the money. It was right there in a large envelope marked with her name. He picked it up and stuffed it into his shirt. He hoped it was enough to get him home, but didn't want to take the time to count it now. Slipping out of the garage, he moved back down the drive to the gate, knowing from what Alistair had said that more people would be coming in soon.

It occurred to him about halfway down the drive who Paula Cook was. He paused just long enough to consider going back to the house and setting them straight on her name being Paula Isaac, but decided that doing that now would get him caught and they'd take his money. He had plans for however much was there.

Getting out of the gates was much easier than going in. He simply waited until the gates opened, then waved at the person coming in as he took off down the road. He didn't even bother with gathering his stuff up, but left it there for whoever wanted it. He laughed aloud when he thought of the giant wolves getting into the bag, and wondered how on earth they'd get the little sticks open. He was nearly home free.

His first stop was at a gas station. He asked for the key and was handed a large tire with it attached. Lance nearly told them to forget it, but he wanted to wash his face and count his money. He dragged the thing with him as he went inside.

He washed his hands and face and thought it felt so good that he did it twice more just because it had been so long. Then after making sure the door was locked three times, he sat on the floor and pulled out the envelope. He was still counting it when someone knocked on the door. Christ, there had to be over ten thousand dollars in the thing. He snarled at the person on the other side of the door to give him a fucking minute.

When he finished counting, he had just under twelve grand, and all of it in cash. He was dancing around the bathroom when the person knocked again. Feeling pretty good about life in general, he didn't even say anything to the man and the little boy as he moved out past them. He decided to have a nice night in a hotel with hot running water. Then a nice juicy steak. But first, he needed clothes befitting his new station.

The suits were nice, but what he really wanted was one that was tailored to his body. Of course, this place wouldn't do it correctly, but he did think about it. In the end, he had to settle for one off the rack and paid out the nearly two thousand for it, thinking the place was selling things entirely too cheaply. He thought when this was all over he might come back here just to have suits made. The price would be worth it.

He rented a cheap hotel room for the night simply to shower and change into his new clothes. He thought about saving his money and staying there, but shrugged that off almost as quickly as it entered his mind. He was going places, and this place wasn't taking him there. After tossing his dirty clothes in the dumpster just outside his rooms, he hailed a cab to the nicest hotel he could think of. Fortunately for him, this little town had one.

The hotel was a little harder to come by. He didn't want to use his own name, but they insisted that they needed a form of identification. Finally, he'd been able to convince the woman that he'd been through hell in the past few days with his wallet being stolen, and could pay a nice deposit if it would make her happy. The manager that she'd called had told him not to worry, but if he would please contact the local police and let them know, they would be fine. He smiled as he went to the elevator, thinking that was never going to happen if he had anything to say about it.

He ordered room service and had a thick juicy steak with a baked potato and all the trimmings, along with a good bottle of wine, and strawberries and cream for dessert. He was about to call his mom and tell her of his good fortune when the news came on about the murder of two people in a parking garage.

Lance watched it in silence, thinking about what he was going to do with all the money he got from the settlement. Allyson was finally beginning to pay off. Lying back on the bed, he decided to surprise his mother and simply show up. He was asleep before the news replayed the news article again.

CHAPTER 14

Ally sat very still and tried not to think about the fact that they were thousands of feet in the air in a long tube. She looked down at her hands, thinking how sore her fingers were going to be when they finally landed, because she couldn't make them let go of the cushion they were gripping, like that was the only thing that was going to save them as they plunged to the ground in a ball of flames. She looked up when someone laughed.

"You should know that your chances of survival are better in a plane than they are on the ground." She rolled her eyes at Alistair. "I'm serious. Besides, I have an insurance policy on you and I can't collect if I'm with you."

"Very funny, asshole." She tried to pull her hands free again and was met with resistance. "You should be trying to make me forget that I think we're going to die rather than making fun of me. I told you I hate to fly."

"So you did. Fifty-three times on the way over here, and at least that many when we got on board." He grinned at her. "Do you really want me to make you forget?"

She nodded, and he stood up. How he did that was beyond her. She could barely sit on this couch like it was in their living room, much less walk around the thing. When he reached for her, she shook her head. When he knelt down in front of her, she nearly cried.

"I can't do this," she said. He nodded. "I really can't. Can you please have them land this thing so I can get off?"

"No. I can't do that, but I can help you." He pushed her back on the couch firmly. "But you'll have to trust me. I can make you forget you're anywhere but with me."

"You have a drug with you?" She was willing to take whatever he had at this point. "I had a little wine before we left so I don't know if whatever you have will...Alistair!"

He ran his hands up her thighs and under her skirt. His hands curled into her panties, and she felt him tear them from her. Her body caught fire that quickly.

"You don't need a drug. You need to relax." She shook her head. "You don't think I can make you relax?"

"I don't think I'm in the mood for sex right now. I'm too nervous to think about anything but dying right now." He moved to his knees, opened her legs, and stood between them. "I'm seriously terrified right now."

"I know. I can feel it. Let me try, baby." He unbuttoned her blouse and ran his hands over her ribs, then slipped his fingers under her bra. "You're so warm. And soft. I love the way your skin feels."

He licked her belly button, then up along her ribs to her bra. It seemed to open on its own. She had a second to wonder if he had torn it from her before he took her nipple into his hot mouth. Then she felt his hands on her bare bottom.

"I want to taste you." She nodded. "But you have to help me, love. I can't get your skirt off if you're holding onto the sofa like this."

She let go, and he lifted her hips and pulled her skirt off, along with her ruined panties. Next, her blouse and bra came off so that she lay before him, naked but for her high heels. He looked at her like she was a meal he was about to devour. And she was pretty sure she was.

His mouth seemed to be everywhere at once. He nipped her at her waist, then at her breast. Her throat was on fire from his tongue laving her, and her nipples felt as if he'd suckled them hard enough to make the blood fill just the tip. She moaned when he cupped her ass and lifted her from the seat.

"Alistair, please. Don't tease me anymore. I need you." She moaned when he lifted his head and looked at her. His cat was racing along his skin and it made her own cat want to play as well.

"I'm not teasing you, Ally. I'm marking you. You have no idea how much having another man's scent on you drives me crazy. My cat wants to mark you, as well, but not here. When we land, I'm going to take you to the nearest woods, and I'm going to let him fuck you until you can't walk. But now he needs a bit of you." She nodded. "Don't scream."

Scream? Then he shifted. His cat lay between her legs and looked at her. Her heart started to pound so hard she was sure he could hear it. Then he put his paw on her waist and held her as he lowered his head to her.

His tongue was rough and thick. Each time he entered her she felt it as if he was fucking her. She couldn't breathe past what he was doing to her, and when he nipped gently at her clit, she came apart, grabbing a pillow and shoving into her mouth. She screamed out her release. She looked down when she felt the air around her tighten and saw Alistair pulling her to the floor.

"I can't wait." He entered her hard, his cock as thick as the tongue that had made her see stars. When Alistair nuzzled her throat, she bared it for him, giving him whatever he wanted so that he'd bring her over the edge again and again.

"Come for me. Now Ally, come now." Her body did as he commanded and bowed up off the carpeted floor. She felt as if she hung there for what seemed an eternity until she came.

Every cell in her body exploded.

Then he sank his teeth into her shoulder, and she came again, screaming out his name and her release over and over until she couldn't move. He didn't let her go, he didn't let her fall to the earth, but kept pounding into her until she felt her body respond again, her need coiling up in her as if she'd not just shattered into a million pieces several times. His command to come again had her soaring up and falling over twice more before he joined her. His body arched over hers, and she watched his cat move along his skin as he roared. She felt her body as it seemed to move away from her and she slid into unconsciousness. Christ, he'd killed her, she thought with a smile.

When she woke, she was lying on a bed. Sitting up, she realized she could hear a shower running. It took her several seconds to realize they were still on the plane. When Alistair stepped out of the bathroom with just a towel around his waist, she licked her lips.

"No. Behave." He grinned at her. "If we weren't landing in like thirty minutes, I'd oblige you, but we are and I can't. Christ, do you have any idea how delicious you look?"

"Your cat...I've never...have you...." She looked away, embarrassed. "I never thought that we could do that. Our animals taking each other like that."

"Neither did I." He sat on the bed. "Look at me, Ally. Please, if I hurt you or...if you don't want me to do that to you again, I never will. I'm so sorry that I let him have you, but he had been pounding against my skin since we left the house."

"I didn't say I didn't like it." He grinned at her outburst. "I just meant isn't that sort of…I don't know…weird?"

"Did you enjoy it?" She nodded and smiled at him. "Then there was nothing weird about it. We're a mated couple, and so are our cats. He needed you, and rather than let us shift at thirty thousand feet, I let him have you before he shifted in a busy airport and ran you down to the ground. Like I said, he could smell the other cats on you, and he wasn't all that happy about it."

She'd hugged his brothers and Jed before they had left yesterday. They needed to go and set things up for them, and she and Alistair were to arrive today to make sure things went according to plan. She was afraid for them all, and she was pretty sure they all knew it.

"He took all that money you planted. Are you sure Lance won't just take off to another country and forget about me and the insurance?" He shook his head as he got up to dress. "Why not?"

"Because he's a greedy prick. Did you hear what he'd done with some of the money already?" She shook her head. "He bought a suit. Not a cheap one, either, but one that cost nearly two grand. Then the shoes and other things needed to make him look good for another thousand. He's a man who likes money too much not to try and come back and get more. Besides, I think he's a little off his rocker. He spoke to his mother yesterday, and she is as bad as him. Probably the reason he's like he is."

She could believe that. His mother was as nasty as they came, and money and the appearance of having a great deal of it meant the world to her. Opening her suitcase, she pulled on a pair of jeans and a pretty t-shirt she'd gotten right before they'd left. She still didn't understand how they had made him believe she was dead and no one else, so she asked him.

"We were following him, and when he got to the first hotel room to, as we now know, clean up for the second one, Keith slipped in and set up the television so that when he turned it on, the news feed we'd had made would tell him about your death. The newspaper was easy, too. But as far as we know, he'd never seen it."

He sounded disappointed in that, and she laughed. "And his mother? How did she know about it? Or did you do the same with her?"

"Same, but we had to have help from Troy on that one. He's the one who made the one here, too. Did you know he owns a newspaper?" He sat down to pull on his shoes and looked at her. "He won't hurt you, love. Not ever again. The man is going to spend the rest of his life and then some in prison for what he's done and what he's planning. Setting up your murder is the least of his problems. He killed that woman Paula."

She nodded. She believed him to a certain point, but she knew Lance better than anyone. He did not like to lose. She sat on Alistair's lap and held him to her breast. She was afraid and didn't want anyone else to get hurt. When the pilot announced for them to take their seats, she looked down at her husband, shocked.

"We're on the plane." He nodded and grinned at her. "You made me...I forgot. I simply forgot to be afraid of dropping out of the sky."

He stood up with her in his arms. "That was the plan. And you're much more relaxed than you were before, too. I know I am."

He purred when she rubbed behind his ear as he took her to the open area and set her on the couch. After making sure she was buckled in, he buckled himself in and pulled her to him for a hungry long kiss. When he lifted his head, she heard the pilot telling them what the weather was like and that he hoped they enjoyed their ride. She flushed and Alistair laughed.

~~~

Alistair watched the two men as they talked about the plan. He also kept an eye on Troy. The man had not said a single word since they'd come into his son's office. But he was sure he had plenty to say.

"You and your wife will be in here during the confrontation with Mr. Isaac. Then when he is arrested, if there is substantial evidence found on him we will allow you to speak to him." The FBI agent looked up at him as if he was going to do just what he'd said.

"I don't think so." The man, Gail Zimmerman, started to open his mouth when Alistair cut him off. "You wouldn't even have him this close if I hadn't alerted you to what was going on. So you'll just sit this out and do things my way."

"I'm a federal officer, and you'll do what—"

"Then we tell him." Zimmerman looked at the other two agents with him before he stood up and glared at him. "You let me do this my way, or my brother lets all parties know that this is a setup."

"You can't do that." Alistair lifted a brow at his tone. "If you do, I'll have you arrested. You'll never see the light of day again."

"On what grounds?" He nodded at Bronwyn, who was sitting very quietly on the couch next to the door. When the doors locked, a loud click sounded in the room, and every agent took a step toward it with their hands going toward their guns.

"I wouldn't do that if I were you. Bronwyn is very powerful, and she's not been in the best of moods since you told her that she couldn't have the air turned up." He winked at her. "She's a very lovely woman, but she doesn't really care for you."

"That's very true. I think you're a pompous ass wipe who needs to take it down a notch or two or I'll…." She turned to Ally. "What did you come up with as a planned threat? I loved it."

"I'll bitch slap you in the nuts and then stomp them. I'm still working on one that works for both sexes. But that one works in this case." Bronwyn nodded and repeated it back to Zimmerman before she smiled again.

"You expect me to believe a woman as far along in her pregnancy as she appears to be could even attempt to take me on?" Zimmerman laughed. "Get real. You're just pissed off because you couldn't handle this on your own so you had to call in the—"

He screamed. As he dropped to the floor, so did the two men who had drawn for their guns. Zimmerman was cupping his balls so tightly that Alistair was sure that the man was going to hurt himself more before Bronwyn was through with him. He walked around the table and knelt in front of the fallen agent.

"She can be a bit on the vicious side when you piss her off. You'll notice that two of your men aren't helping you. Would you like to know why?" He cried out his answer, and Alistair looked at them. They both nodded before he answered the man. "They're not human, like we're not."

"What the fuck are you talking about?" Zimmerman looked around the room. "She might not be, but when she lets me go I'm going to show her what I'm about."

The shift from human to cat was almost instantaneous, and there was no stopping Ryland either. He tossed the man to the floor and had his giant paw planted on his chest so quickly that he was sure the man didn't even get a chance to take a deep breath.

"And this is my brother, Ryland. You should know that he doesn't care for you much, either. And he said to tell you if you speak about his wife that way again, he will not just bitch slap your balls for you but tear them from your body with his teeth." Ryland snarled his agreement, and Alistair reached up and rubbed his hand along his fur. "You still think we can't handle a human who's hurt one of us?"

"Is he going to eat me?" Alistair looked at Ryland, who turned to look at him. He heard his brother's laughter, and was fighting hard not to join him. He looked back at Zimmerman, who was still staring at the tiger on him with wide eyes.

"I don't know. He seems to think you owe us all an apology...and a special one to his wife." Ryland backed off, but not before he tore the man's shirt open. There was no blood, but there were deep marks that would hurt for some time.

Zimmerman lay there and glared at the two men who were still standing. They were going to be out of a job before this was over, and Alistair felt badly for them. When Zimmerman stood up, he walked to Bronwyn and bowed before her.

"I'm terribly sorry, Mrs. Golden. I had no idea that you were...were...whatever you are. And your husband...." He shivered and turned to look at the tiger that came to stand beside him. "I had no idea that he could...."

He sat down hard and held his head. Bronwyn nodded, put her hand on Zimmerman's head, and held him while

Ryland moved to the bathroom. Brock tossed a bag in there with him and pulled the door closed. In seconds the room was set to rights and the two human agents were set on a chair. Zimmerman was the only one that was left on the floor. When Bronwyn let him go, he looked around the room, dazed.

"What happened?" Alistair shrugged, not giving the man any clue of what had just happened to him. "I had…my head hurts and…did I fall?"

"You did. I think you tripped over your own feet when you were telling us that you think Alistair's plan works much better." Bronwyn sat back down and fanned herself. "Do you think it would be possible for the air to be turned up a bit? I'm sorry, but I'm roasting over here."

Zimmerman asked Marcus if that would be possible. Marcus nodded and looked at his dad. Troy was laughing so hard that tears were streaming down his face, but he nodded and reached behind him to adjust the thermostat.

Ryland came out of the bathroom dressed again and was adjusting his tie when he put out his hand to help Zimmerman up. The man whimpered, and Troy lost control of his mirth. It was infectious laughter, and soon the room was joining him.

"Oh my, I'm going to enjoy this," he said. "I surely am. You and I are going to have a talk when this little thing is over. I have something I'd like to discuss with you and your family."

Alistair nodded, not sure what the man wanted, but wanting to get this going. He looked at his wife and she shrugged. He smiled when she did, and they continued with the plan. An hour before Isaac was supposed to land back in his home state, everyone was in agreement as to what was going to happen. The agents, along with the two officers that were assigned to help them, left a few minutes later. Alistair turned to Bronwyn.

"He was going to tell. Everything, and when he was through, he had plans of getting with an agent friend of his who has some paperwork on me that works for the CIA." Bronwyn stood up to pace. "He doesn't know it's about me or us, but he knows that this man believes there is a woman who can change into a tiger. He wants to bring me in and have me tested."

"Did you get a name?" She nodded at Troy, who suddenly stopped laughing. "You tell me and I'll see what I can do about getting to the bottom of it before anyone else finds you. No one will touch you as long as I'm around."

"His name is Sheldon Pierce, and he works in CIA in Files. He has the papers at his home, or I guess copies of them." Bronwyn looked at him. "I'm sorry, Alistair. I was only going to erase his memory about the two men with him so he wouldn't hurt their career when I found that. He can't know about us. It's too dangerous."

"It is, love, and you did the right thing. I can't stand the fact that this other man knows as much as he thinks he does. But for now you're safe." She nodded, and Ryland pulled her into his arms. "We have to finish this with Isaac. Then we'll work on Zimmerman and the other man. Everyone in agreement with that?" They all nodded and sat down to go over what they were going to do to Isaac and his mother. Things were about to go badly for the two of them.

By the time they were called to say that Isaac was on the ground, they were headed to their points of the plan. Troy, Marcus, Ally, and himself sat in the office waiting for the shit to hit the fan.

"This is going to be so much fun. That man isn't going to know what happened to him." Troy laughed as he continued. "Yes, sir, best fun I've had in some time."

169

CHAPTER 15

Lance hated his trip. Not even being in first class had made his trip worth ever going commercial again. He was going to have to see about getting his jet back as soon as he collected on his policy. He held his one case in his hand as he left the plane, snarling at the stewardess that wished him a good day.

"Stupid cunt," he said, just loud enough for her to hear, and smiled when he heard her sharp intake of breath. He would never see her again and didn't care if she was pissed off. He was on his own turf now. Fuck her.

He had to rent a car because his limo was no longer available to him. The woman behind the counter told him that the company he had requested had refused to come for him until he paid his past due balance. He told her to call someone else, and wasn't really surprised to hear that none of them would help him. Lance had a feeling she was telling them he had a large balance with another firm and that was why he had to drive himself rather than ride like was befitting his station.

He'd not driven a car much…rarely, if ever, did he find the need to take himself somewhere when a car with a driver could take him there in comfort. Lance hated everything about the car and driving the thing through traffic. He was sure that everyone on the road knew that he wasn't as well versed as he usually was in driving, and set out to make his life a living hell. It was all right. Soon, he'd have his money and they'd all wish they'd treated him better.

He drove to his house, only to find there was a notice nailed to the door saying that it had been seized for nonpayment of taxes. He wasn't sure how that came to be when he felt that taxes were beneath him, but didn't know where to find his mother if she wasn't there. He was ready to pull out his new cell phone when someone came up the drive on a little motor bike.

"You Mr. Lance Isaac?" The kid, who couldn't have been more than sixteen, stood there with his pants hanging to his knees and his hat turned to its side. "I got a message here, if you are. If not, then say so. I don't have all damned day."

"Who is it from?" The kid shrugged and told him to fucking sign for it and he could find out himself. "You're a rude fuck, and I'm going to tell your company."

Lance snatched the envelope and scribbled "fuck off" on the signature line. The kid read it and laughed as he flipped Lance off and drove away. He opened the envelope and read what it said.

"Darling, I heard you were coming home, and as I had no way to contact you, I had to have someone watch for you. You should have called me. I'm staying at the hotel on Winding Green Way. Come there. I'm in suite seventeen."

Suite? How the hell is she affording that, he wondered as he got back into his car and made his way back into town. He was just parking the car when he realized that his mother had been holding out on him. She was staying in the best hotel in their town, and in a suite as well. She had a great deal of explaining to do when he saw her.

He went to the elevator and nearly fell over his own feet when he saw the woman come out as the door opened. He turned to follow her when she was swept up into the arms of another man. He had been sure it was Ally.

As the doors opened on the seventeenth floor, he knocked on the door in front of him and waited for someone to answer it. When his mother did, she looked completely surprised to see him there.

"How did you find me?" He quirked a brow at her. "You gave me no way to contact you, and here you show up like you knew just where I was. How did you know?"

"You told me." He moved in the room to see that it suited her…and him. He thought that living there would be a great deal more advantageous than a house. For one thing, someone cleaned it daily and made his bed. He'd not had that luxury for some time.

"I did no such thing. I only moved in here yesterday, and I've not spoken to you since before that. How did you find out?" He handed her the crumbled note, sat down in front of her lunch tray, and opened the covered plates.

"This looks good." He picked up the fork and took a mouthful of her salad. "I don't care for this dressing, but I'll eat it all the same. What are you having?"

She sat down and shoved the note back at him. "This isn't my handwriting. You should know that. Do you know whose is it?"

"Yours. Don't fuck around, Mother. I'm tired and I want to eat. You should have some of this salmon. It's delicious."

"I was planning on it. Why are you eating my dinner? Order your own." She tried to take the plate from him, but he wasn't having it. She glared at him before she finally gave up.

"I want to know how you're affording all this." He took another bite of the asparagus and moaned. "Unless you had a stash hiding away, you've done something you shouldn't have."

"What about you? You're dressed better than I've seen you dressed in a while, and you seem to smell of good fortune. And you never answered me about the handwriting. Do you know who this is?"

"As I said, it's yours. Why do you care anyway? It's not like both of us haven't been dealing the other dirty." He leaned back when he'd finished most of the meal. "And if it's not yours, whose handwriting it is?"

"It's Allyson's." He felt his skin pale and tried to think. He took the note when she handed it back to him and looked at it carefully.

"How is that possible? She's dead." His mother nodded. "You didn't write this to make me crazy, did you? It's okay if you did, I'll forgive you."

"I didn't do it. It's sick and…where did you get it? You said I gave it to you, and we both know I didn't. So where did you get this?"

"A kid rode up on this motorcycle and handed it to me. Flipped me off, too, and had me sign for it." He looked at the note again. "I thought the handwriting looked familiar, and I suppose in a way it does, but I never thought it was Allyson's."

He sat there for several minutes, not listening to his mother as she prattled on about insurance and having her sign off on other things as well. Then he looked up at her when she mentioned the appointment she had.

"When?" She looked slightly panicky, and he realized she'd just been emptying her head again, not really paying any attention to what she'd been saying. "When is the appointment with the insurance claims adjustor?"

"This evening. I'm supposed to meet him in the bar downstairs." Before he could ask her why she was meeting him, she continued. "You said you weren't coming back, and I have to have something to live on. I told him you were killed in Ohio and that I was your only living heir. He had to have a death certificate and…well, I used your father's and made a few minor changes on it. He didn't even flinch when I handed it to him."

"So you faked my death." She nodded and started to stand up. He wasn't sure where she thought she was going now, but she wasn't going to claim his money. He had plans for that money, and none of them included her.

"What would you have had me do? Let the IRS take everything we had and live with strangers in an apartment building like cockroaches in the walls?" She snorted. "Oh please. I wouldn't live in one of those large pest-invested boxes if that was all I could afford. I deserve more, and you owe it to me."

"*I* owe it to you? How do you figure that? And as for everything you had, everything in that house belonged to me. You moved in because your husband had put a bullet in his head rather than to tell you *no*. You ever think you might have been the reason he was so fucking broke that he had not even a pot to piss in? It was a good thing that he'd paid off his funeral before he killed himself or you would have put him in a box in the back yard rather than go to the expense of putting him away like he wanted." She slapped him across the face, and he grabbed her around the throat before she could back away. "You touch me again and I will kill you."

She struggled with him, and he let her go and went back to the table to think. She had had him declared dead. He wasn't sure that was going to hurt him or help him right now. He looked around the room again, and wondered if he let her go and get his money how long would it be before someone found her body after he killed her. He decided not long, and looked at her as she glared at him from across the room.

"You're going to go and get the money, and we'll split it and go our separate ways after that." She started to open her mouth when he held up his hand. "Or I go get the money and leave your dead body in here for the maid service to find a week from now."

"You'd kill your own mother?"

"In a heartbeat."

"You're a horrible man, Lance Isaac. What would your father think of the way you're treating me?"

"He'd probably tell me *thank you*." He leaned back in the chair. Either way, he would win. She just didn't know that he wasn't going to split anything with her, and the service would find her in a few days, not a week.

"I'll do this your way, but I want you to know that I hate you right now." He nodded. "I'm supposed to have my hair done in an hour. You'll have to hide back there. Janet is coming here to do it so I'll look nice."

He only nodded. When she offered her cheek as he walked by her, he ignored it. He was not leaving any DNA on her if at all possible. A single bullet to the head and she'd no longer be a problem. He just had to find a gun now.

~~~

Ally had been nervous that Lance would hit her when she exited the elevator, but all he'd done was stare at her. She had moved to Alistair's arms, and they both had moved away. Now she was sitting in the bar waiting with Ryland while Lance negotiated a deal for a gun. She had her back to him. And when Ryland nodded, she stood up and walked by his table, stumbling a little as she'd been told to do. She smiled as she headed to the men's room, where Alistair was waiting for her. Lance had seen her again.

"This is going to drive him insane." Alistair nodded and kissed her.

"What's next? Do I get to serve him a drink?"

"Getting into this now, are you?" He laughed. "No, but you are going to see him a few more times. Wait here while I go see if you can move yet."

When he returned, she walked on his left as they walked by the table where an employee of Troy's was sitting, pretending to be a gun dealer. He nodded to the bar, and they hurried by when Lance turned to go back to the table with two beers in his hand. This was becoming fun.

The plan was to drive him over the edge. She wasn't sure that he wasn't already there, but she thought it was a good plan. Bronwyn had told her that she'd done something like this when someone had tried to kidnap her. She'd faked her own death, then haunted him for weeks after. He'd finally confessed to what he'd done, and she had moved to another city. He'd never bothered her again.

When she and Alistair had headed back to their room, she saw Troy and Marcus coming out of their room. She felt sorry for the two men. They'd lost so much, and now they were dealing with the man again. She hoped that when they exhumed their child…and Paula had been a child to them both…that they would find just what they needed to get justice for her death.

"We were just going on. Donny just called to let us know that he and Isaac had left the hotel and were en route to get the gun." Marcus laughed as the continued. "Hopefully the fool is as stupid as we think he is and won't bother with checking the gun out too closely when Donny gives it to him."

It was a prop. It would fire, make all the correct sounds and actions, but it wouldn't shoot anything but blanks. And when Donny sold it to Lance, it would be loaded with them, as would the box of extras that Lance had insisted that he might need. He was spending nearly three thousand dollars on this gun as well as quiet money for Donny.

"We were about to have dinner, too." She glanced at Alistair when he told them that. "Would you mind if we joined you? My family is going to be down there, too, if you don't mind a noisy crowd."

Marcus looked at his dad, but she could see that he really wanted to join them. Ally liked both men, but she had a special place in her heart for Troy. He was the grandfather she'd never had. When Troy nodded, they moved toward the elevator together just as Sandra and Jed came down the hall. By the time the elevator doors opened, all the Golden family was standing with them, as well as a couple who had come from their room at the last second.

"We might be too heavy for one elevator," Ryland said as he looked down at his wife. "I mean, I think there's a weight limit."

"You ass." Bronwyn looked at Marcus when he laughed, then turned it to a hard cough. "You might not want to ride with me, either. There might be blood and mayhem in the one I ride in if my husband comes with me."

"How about we ride on the next one, ladies?" Marcus put out his arm to Bronwyn and Sandra. "That way if their heavy egos—and I have no doubt there is a great deal of that going around—get the better of them, at least we'll be safely in the dining room when they crash to the bottom."

Sandra put her arm through his, and Bronwyn simply nodded. Marcus was still getting used to the no touching rule, but they'd all been working around it with him. He nodded as they stepped in the open doors with the younger couple. As the doors shut, the one next to it opened. As theirs had made a stop, they ended up in the main lobby together. And there, waiting for an elevator, was Aida Isaac.

Ally wasn't sure what to do, but she walked by her without a word. Bronwyn stepped between the two of them just as Aida started to turn and fell against the other woman. She stepped back and smiled at her.

"Sorry. In this advanced state, I'm as clumsy as a beached whale." Aida sniffed hard and looked at Bronwyn as if she had something contagious. "You look familiar, do I know you?"

"I highly doubt we run in the same circles, young woman. My son is a lawyer, and we tend to stick to our own kind." Bronwyn took a step toward the woman, but Ryland wrapped his arm around her shoulders and pulled her back. "There should be special elevators for people like you. I'm in one of the suites, and I think we should have preferential treatment."

"Oh, I agree." Bronwyn looked ready to do harm when the woman turned her back to her. "You should be careful of these regular people elevators. They've been sticking between floors a great deal, I heard." The doors closed before anything more could be said.

Bronwyn stood there for several seconds until they all heard something that sounded a great deal like an elevator stopping suddenly. She grinned at Ryland and started away. He said her name.

"Oh, for heaven's sake, she'll only be in there for an hour or so. It's a hell of a lot better than what I wanted to do to her. At least she can still breathe." She moved toward the dining room and left them all standing there. Ally looked at Alistair and shook her head.

"Remind me never to piss her off. It could be very scary."
Troy laughed. Then the others joined him. Bronwyn only had
a few more weeks to go before the baby was born. Ally hoped
it would calm her a little bit, but she had a feeling it wouldn't.
Smiling as she took Alistair's arm, she wished she was like
her. It could be fun to have others a little afraid of her once in
a while.

Tomorrow was the big showdown, and she knew that
everyone at the table was a little tense about it. So much
could go wrong, and she was betting that some things would.
But she had faith in her family, and that was all that mattered,
she supposed. When Troy sat down beside her, she smiled at
him.

"I'd like to speak to you and Alistair before you go back
home. It's important. I know you two are just starting out
your lives together, but I have something I need from you."
She nodded as he continued. "My son...we're both getting up
there in years, and until Paula died, we had a set plan.
Now...well, now we have devoted our lives to getting that
prick to own up to what he's done. And that, too, seems to be
coming to a head."

Alistair sat down in his seat, seemingly hearing what the
older man had been saying. "Your lives aren't over either,
Troy. You and your son have a great deal to offer others, as
well as the time to do it."

Troy nodded. "That's true, but we need a project. A big
one that will keep us out of trouble, I think. And we'd like for
the two of you to help us with it."

"You know you can depend on us." She looked at
Alistair, and he nodded. "We will do whatever it is you need
us to. If you hadn't called in a few favors, we might not have
gotten Lance and his mother for a few more years...if ever."

"Yes, you would have. You're much too smart to let that prick get away with what he's done to you. We're just lucky that you let us along for the ride. We'd been close to giving up on him and letting it go. It was beginning to take us over, and we realized that our Paula wouldn't have wanted that." He glanced at his son, who nodded at him. "We're going to sell out here, and we want to move to Ohio. Our businesses here can be done from anywhere, and the ranch isn't the same any more. Neither of us have a spouse or anyone to share it with, anyway. What would you say about helping us start up out there? Getting us a house we can live in and some land where we can have you all out to run and have some dinner with two old men?"

"You're serious?" Troy nodded at Alistair. "Well, I can help you with that. I know of a few places that have hit on some hard times that you can get for a good price. I also know of a few buildings that you can lease or buy if you want to extend your businesses out there if the need comes up. What is it you do anyway, if you don't mind my asking?"

Troy laughed. "Marcus is a lawyer like you are. He's been doing it a bit longer, however, but he wants to retire. I'm...well...I buy things. I love go to auctions and pick up a few things, and maybe flip them if I decide I no longer need it or want it. You might say it's my passion. We can do that most anywhere, I guess. And out in your neck of the woods would be a different thing for us. You know we have a ranch house we've had forever, and it's time to go to something a little smaller. You have anything we can maybe move in sooner rather than later?"

Alistair nodded. "Yes. As a matter of fact, there's a house not far from the downtown area that's pretty close to our home. If you're thinking you want to live closer to the city, I think I can do that as well."

"Your home is good. That way we can become sort of foster-grandparents to the little ones when they come. If you don't mind." They both nodded. "Good. We'll put our home on the market in the morning."

As he walked away, Ally looked at Alistair. "What just happened here? Did we gain a dad and granddad for our children we don't have yet, as well as a neighbor? Or did I miss something?"

"Nope. I think we just got adopted." He kissed her on the nose. "Do you mind? I mean, I really like them both, and they seem to be lonely. I just have to figure out if they can afford to live out here while their house sells. Maybe they might want to think that over a bit before they get in over their heads by having two houses they might not be able to afford."

She nodded. She supposed they really were lonely if they were going to simply pick up and leave like they were.

CHAPTER 16

The law firm of Kibble and James was sitting in the hotel conference room when Alistair and Ryland walked in. Neal was also joining them, as well as Troy and Marcus. Alistair wasn't sure why they'd been invited, but he really didn't care. They had three hours before they confronted Lance.

He smiled as he got himself a glass of iced tea. Ally had run into Lance as they were walking the lobby toward the elevators last night. He had turned and run after her, but she'd stepped into the elevator before he could find her again. She had laughed for hours about it. Just once more and he'd know that he'd fucked up royally. Then this meeting had been called.

"Good morning, gentlemen." Neal sat as soon as he came in the room and looked around. "I don't know what this is all about, but if it has anything to do with what has happened with your firm and Lance Isaac, I'm not sure why you requested that I be here. I'm just the accountant for my family's firm and personal accounts."

One of the men that had requested the meeting stood. "My name is John Kibble, and this is my partner, Able James. We're here because of another matter, though we'd like to be kept in the loop with Isaac as well. We've been called to help smooth the way for you to take over the finances for one of our clients. Mr. and Mr. Cook have informed us that you are the man that's going to do it."

Neal looked at him, then at Ryland. None of them seemed to have a clue what they were talking about. He stood up when John handed each of them a thick file. He didn't even look at it, because he was sure there was some sort of misunderstanding.

"While I did talk with Mr. Cook last night about him moving his residence to Ohio, I don't know what this is all about." He looked at the two men in question. "You want us to take care of your finances, too?"

"Of course. We'll need money, won't we? And these two have been our attorneys for...well hell, John, how long you been working for me? Nearly fifty years, I think, right?"

John smiled at Troy as he answered him. "More like seventy. And you've been our only clients for nearly the last ten. It's about time you got off your ass and found someone younger. I've been telling you for years that we want to go fishing."

Neal looked at the file that he'd been handed, and then at Troy. He looked pole axed. He picked up the file and glanced over the first sheet, then sat down as what it said occurred to him.

"You're not poor at all." Marcus laughed, and Alistair felt his face heat. "I was going to speak to you when this was over to see if you could afford to have two houses if the one here didn't sell. But I guess...Christ, you're worth billions more than we are."

"Course we are. We've been around a little longer than you." Troy took the file from him and put it on the table before he spoke again. "We know this is a great deal to take on, but you did say you'd help us."

Alistair nodded, not sure what else to do. "You really don't think…. We just handle our own issues. We aren't…I'm not up to the kind of money that you're talking about here. Are you?" He looked at Neal who shook his head, then nodded.

"I may not be now, but I'd be willing to bet I can learn pretty fucking quick." He smiled at Troy. "You weren't born rich, either, were you? You made every penny of this by hard work and sweat. You wear money like it wasn't given to you but you earned it. I love that about you."

Able nodded. "They have worked very hard for this money and will continue to do so. Marcus will call you in the middle of the night about a deal he wants to try, and by the time most people are rolling out of bed, he's doubled his money. The man has a knack."

Alistair looked at Ryland. who hadn't said anything. It would be his decision, and he was pretty sure that the four men that wanted this to work knew it, too. As he put the file on the table, Alistair held his breath. Ryland looked at each of them before he spoke.

"You're not going to be able to find better or more honest men to help you. My family prides itself on their integrity and honesty." Marcus nodded, as did Troy. "But what you're asking us to do, because it does involve us all, is well beyond what we're used to. What is it you think you'll get out of this?"

"Honest men, as you said. Men who will work for us and not expect us to work for you." Marcus looked at his dad before he continued. "We can do all this on our own. We can invest and put our money in the right places, but we also want to be able to have our bit of fun. As Dad told you last night, he loves auctions. He enjoys the play and the payoff, if there is any. I want to paint, I want to learn to sculpt and do things I thought I never had time for before. I want to…. My daughter died, murdered by a man who met her through our business dealings and took her life because he thought he could make a few bucks off her. We need to live because she didn't get to."

Ryland nodded and looked at him and Neal. "You do what you want, and you'll have my support. I know you both can do this, and if you think any differently, I suggest you tell them no. But you can."

Alistair looked at Neal. It would be their work that would make or break this deal. And when Neal nodded, he looked at the other men. "We'll do it. As soon as you get a contract together, we'll look it over and—" Another set of files slid across the table at them.

"There's our contract. You read it over and get back to us." Able smiled as he looked at John, then back at them. "Like I said, we've been telling them to do this for some time and have had this contract ready, except for the names, for just as long. We'll take care of the sale of the house here, and you take care of the one on your end. There are some specs they would like to have, so if you know of any, send me the pictures and the real-estate office's name, and I'll show them. Marcus and Troy will see to their household here. And once you have found them a house, they'll close up here and move. I've already got a buyer for their home, so it is just a matter of getting their things sent before they will leave here."

John and Able asked if they had any questions. Alistair told them that he didn't right now, but he might in an hour. They told him that they'd be there for them for as long as they were still landlocked. But they already had their boat packed and were ready to head out to sea.

"You really want this to happen?" Troy nodded to him. "I don't understand. There is any number of firms much larger than us that could and would do this for you that have a great deal more experience than we have."

"You're right, but they don't have the heart we can see in you and your family." Marcus sat down and picked up a pen and a sheet of paper. "What do you see here, Alistair? Don't put too much thought into it. Just tell me what you see."

He said the first thing that popped into his head. "Potential. Or a clean slate."

"I like your first answer. And you're right. Potential is what we see when we look at what you and your family can do for us." Marcus lay the paper down and stood. "You know what else I see? A man who didn't ask what we could do for him."

The men left, and Alistair sat there looking at the blank sheet of paper. What the fuck had he gotten himself into? He looked up when the door to the conference room opened and Ally stepped inside.

"Your brother said you might need me." He nodded. "I was taking a bath when he touched my mind. It was a little weird having him do that at that time. Ryland needs to have a little bell that goes off when…what's happened?"

"Nothing." She looked at him oddly, and he smiled. "Nothing at all. I was just sitting here thinking that after today I'm going to have you all for myself."

"That could be bad for you. I'm not one for being idle. I was thinking of getting a job. Did you know I have a law degree, too?" He didn't but was glad to hear it. "I was thinking of seeing if I could work for one of the firms downtown to see if I have what it takes."

He pulled her onto his lap. "I have a job for you. One I think you're going to be very good at. What do you think about working for me?"

~~~

Lance sat in the chair in his mother's suite and tried to think about what he'd seen last night. He was sure it had been Allyson, but he knew that couldn't be right. She was more than likely buried by now. He looked up at his mother who came out of the other bedroom.

"You should know that I hate that you're staying here. Why can't you find somewhere else to stay? I think the staff is wondering where I'm putting all the food I'm ordering. And if you think I'm paying for what you eat, you're nuts." She fussed with her blouse as she glared. "As soon as I get my part of the money, I'm going to have a nice, long vacation. I'm thinking I'll take one of those long European cruises."

He wasn't required to answer, so he didn't. "Have you seen anything odd in the past few days? Like…I don't know…someone from our past?"

He knew she had the moment she looked at him. She looked at the door as if she expected someone to come through it, and he nearly did as well. But she shook her head and stood up.

"Allyson. I thought…two days ago I thought I saw her when I was getting on the elevator. You remember the time I was stuck in that dreadful thing for an hour before anyone would come and get me out?" He nodded, thinking it had been the quietest hour he'd ever enjoyed. "That woman had something to do with it, I know."

"Allyson made you stuck in the elevator?" She huffed at him and sat down. He wasn't sure he wanted to hear about her mishap in the elevator again because he heard about it for nearly three hours the day before.

"No, the woman who looked like she was about to explode she was so large with her child. Why women want to flaunt that is beyond me. She should have simply stayed at home if she wanted to get herself knocked up like that. I mean really, who wants to see that anyway? She simply let herself go and now expects—"

"Mother. Tell me about Allyson." She huffed again, and he thought he was going to have to kill her before her meeting with the insurance adjustor. She sat back and looked at him.

"Why? Is she coming back to haunt you, as well?" He felt the finger of fear he'd felt the day before slide down his spine. "She's dead. We both know it. What are you afraid of?"

That she wasn't dead and that today was a trap. But if it was a trap, why show herself to him? And whoever it had been had not been coy about him seeing her but had practically went out of her way so he could see her. He rubbed his hand over his face and tried to relax. Just twenty-five more minutes and his mom would go and get the check. And an hour after that, he'd be a rich man again.

She stood up and reached for her purse, and he stood as well. This was going to be tricky. He was going with her, but he knew she wasn't going to like it. When she went to the door, he was right behind her.

"Where do you think you're going?" He nodded to the door. "You can't go with me. He thinks you're dead. If you show up, we'll get nothing. And I fucking want this money."

"As do I. But if you think I'm going to let you collect it without keeping an eye on you, you're stupider than that cow of a woman you were talking about." She looked like she was going to argue with him, but he simply crossed his arms over his chest and glared at her. "I'm going whether you like it or not."

The ride down to the lobby was made in silence. She moved through the lobby like she was on a mission, and he grinned at her behind her back. When she entered the dining room, he followed. The man who was there wouldn't know who he was, so he didn't bother hiding from him. Ordering lunch and having it charged to his mother's room, he waited for the man to hand his mother the check. Soon, this would be all over and he'd be a free man. He looked up when someone sat down across from him.

"Do I know you?" The man shook his head and looked over at his mother and the man that was going over something with her. "Then I'd very much like it if you got the hell up from my table and found your own. I'm trying to have lunch here."

"You're watching to make sure she doesn't rob you blind is what you're doing." The fear he'd felt earlier doubled as the man turned back to look at him. "You should know that she isn't going share anything she gets today. That man she's with? He doesn't even work for the company that carries the policy."

Lance started to rise from his seat, but the man laid a gun on the table between them as well as a cell phone. He sat back down. He glanced at his mother as she nodded to whatever was on the sheet in front of her.

"She lied to me." The man grinned. "She set me up. And now she's going to get all my money, and I'll get shit."

"Oh, you'll get shit all right, but so will she. Insurance fraud is a capital offense. And I would have thought you would have known that." Lance nodded but was confused and asked the man what he meant. "The policy is on Allyson Isaac...or I should say Ally Golden, right? She and my brother married about a week ago. I'm Neal, by the way."

Lance nodded, still not sure what was going on. "The policy is up to date, and I have all the receipts to prove it. And my mother is collecting it because Allyson is dead."

"No, she's not." Lance looked around the room. He had a feeling that the woman he'd been seeing was his wife and she'd been playing with him.

"She's here, isn't she? She's come here to fuck with me, and she thinks I'm going to just sit by and let her ruin me?" Neal laughed. "You think this is funny? I have everything riding on that money, and I plan to collect it one way or the other."

"Really? So you think to kill her if she's not really dead." The man tsked. "Not very smart of you, really. I did tell you I'm her brother, right? And as my sister, I will protect her with my life if need be. But I don't think that's going to be necessary, do you?"

Lance looked at the men who just walked in and sat at the table next to his. He knew them. They were the Cook's, his second wives father and grandfather. They both nodded to him as they picked up their menus. Lance looked at Neal.

"They're in on this, as well, I suppose." Neal nodded. "Who else should I expect to walk through the door? Delia's parents? I assure you that I had nothing at all to do with her death."

"But you did Paula's, didn't you? As did your mother." He handed him a sheath of papers and nodded. "You should read those before you answer. It's transcripts of your conversation with your mother. We were able to record everything you said."

He didn't even bother looking at them. They'd not had his permission to record the conversation, and he told the man that. Nothing they had in that could be used against him.

"No, we didn't need yours. We got what we wanted the other way." He looked at his mother when she laughed. "She's a hell of a woman, your mother."

She'd sold him out. He glanced at the papers again and realized that if they let her record even some of the conversations they'd had, he was so fucked. He looked to the door again, wondering if he could make it out of it when Kimble and James both walked in and sat at another table. Both of them looked at him rather than their menus and smiled. Lance looked at Neal.

"Yeah, there's a problem where you work, too. Something about mail fraud and theft, I think. Did you know that overbilling is a capital offense, too? You're batting about two for two right now. Ever hear the term 'three strikes you're out'?" Neal laughed. "I think you better hope no one else comes to have lunch here."

He knew who else was coming through the door, but he planned on being gone before she did. Allyson would be the crowning point in this day. He watched his mother stand and thank the man she was with, and he reached into his pocket for the gun. He'd kill her, take the check, and run. He lifted it just enough under the table to take her out when Allyson stepped to the table his mother and the fake insurance man were at.

Lance figured since he was going to prison anyway, he might as well make it worth his while. He pulled the trigger until he heard the slide click back, and smiled at the man sitting across from him. He was grinning at him, as well.

"I guess she's dead now. I killed myself two wives and am as broke as fuck because no one would pay off. How shitty is that, I ask you?" He laughed again as he put his gun on the table and put his hands up. "I get to go to prison, and there isn't anything you can do to me that they won't inside."

"You might want to have another look around, buddy. You were shooting blanks." Lance didn't look around, because he knew, just knew the man was telling him the truth.

It would be like him to fuck this up, as well. Neal nodded to the room, and Lance turned slowly to see Allyson standing in front of him, smiling. And just behind her, his mother was being put into handcuffs while she cursed a stream of profanities. He looked at the Cooks, who he'd shot at, too, and found them being served their salads. The men from his firm were looking at a magazine as if he'd not just shot them to death…which he supposed he had not.

Alistair came in and sat at the chair next to him, and Allyson on his other side. They both looked entirely too happy. When he lifted his hand to slap the smirk off Allyson's face, she grabbed it and twisted it so that he was in so much pain he cried out. She twisted harder, and he started to lift his other hand when she punched him in the face.

"Doesn't feel too good, does it, Lance? To be helpless when someone else holds you down and makes you hurt?" She told him to answer her, and he seemed to have no choice.

"I never gave you what you didn't crave." She turned his arm again, and he felt his wrist break. "You're fucking going to pay for that, bitch, just as soon as I'm free."

Alistair laughed. "You should realize by now that you're never going to be free, Lance. You're going to be lucky if you only go to prison after what we have on you."

"You have nothing, on me. She's the one that's trying to collect on an insurance policy. You might want to check the law again. I'm as innocent as they come."

Alistair reached down and picked up the phone that Brock had put on the table. After pushing a couple of buttons, his voice screamed back at him. *"I guess she's dead now. I killed myself two wives and am as broke as fuck because no one would pay off. How shitty is that, I ask you?"*

"I think that's a confession." Alistair shut it off just as he was laughing on the recording. "You should know that Neal isn't a professional liar like you, so if you'd have asked him if he was recording your conversation, he would have told you he was. He did tell you that he'd recorded them earlier, and you should have guessed he would do it now."

Lance started laughing. His mother went by the table they were sitting at and spit on him. He didn't even bother wiping it off. He was going to die, and there wasn't a fucking thing either of them could do about it. Laughing, he asked Alistair for a sheet of paper and a pen. Allyson gave him both from her purse. He cleared himself a place and began writing. He was still writing when the police or whatever they were came to ask him a few questions.

"*I, Lance Tyler Isaac, hereby confess to the following crimes,*" the first line said. He wrote until his hand cramped up. Then when they took him to jail, he got to read it all in the camera, and they let him finish his narrative that way. "I killed my first person when I was seventeen. I got her drunk and led her to the beach to rape her…." If he was going to die, he was going to go out in style.

CHAPTER 17

He woke and reached for Ally, but she wasn't there. Again. He sat up and looked around their room and noticed that in addition to her clothes being gone, his were as well, which meant she was washing them. Again.

While he was in the shower, he thought about what she might be going through. He'd asked her several times in the week they'd been back, but she'd told him she was just tired. He was ready to ask Bronwyn to see if there was really something wrong with her. He dressed in causal jeans and a T-shirt, hoping to talk her into going for a ride on the bike. She was sitting in the kitchen alone, staring at nothing he could see with the paper in front of her.

"You hungry?" She looked at him, sort of dazed, and he asked her again. She shook her head. He began pulling out things to make them both something to eat because he knew with Jed gone over to help the Cooks set up their kitchen that she hadn't eaten.

"Why do you love me?" He turned to look at her, but before he could answer, she continued. "Is it because you have to, because we were fated to be mates? Or that you just do? I don't really understand it."

He looked around the room while she sat there. He knew that answering this wrong could hurt her. He noticed the boxes of old appliances in the corner that had been replaced over the past few days.

"Why did you fix this kitchen? The things here worked, but not well. Why did you do that?" He thought it was still wrong, but she seemed to think about it as she looked around, too.

"They were working, but…well, some of them leaked. The toaster needed to be begged to work, and the…." She looked at him and smiled. "I replaced them because I wanted to. For us."

He nodded, hoping she was keeping up with him. "And even though you were able to use the other things there, you felt the need to replace them. Why?"

"Because," she started as she stood up and came to him. "Because I want to make a home with you. I want to be able to come in here even if Jed is here and make you things because you and your family enjoy them. I replaced them because, while they worked, they were not perfect. For you."

He pulled her to him as he leaned against the counter and kissed her. It was soft, and as much as he tried not to show her how hungry he was for her, she gave him her hunger and he moaned. He cupped her ass and brought her against his thickening cock and rocked into her. She pulled away, and his cat nearly snarled at him. They both wanted their mates.

"Sit on the counter." Her voice was rough and low. He stared at her for several seconds, trying to get his mind to wrap around what she'd said to him. "Take off your pants and sit on the counter. I want to take you into my mouth and have you come down my throat."

He nearly hurt himself getting his pants undone, and had his jeans and boxers off in seconds. She pulled his shirt over his head when he was seated on the counter, and he leaned back when she told him to.

"I love you, Alistair." He nodded because she licked his cock from root the tip right then, and he was incapable of breathing, much less talking. "And I will for the rest of our lives."

He curled his hand in her hair as she lowered her head over him. She sucked him so hard he nearly came up off the counter. It felt so fantastic. Every time she suckled at him he lifted his hips up to go deeper, wanting to slide down her incredible throat.

Sweat slid down his spine as she brought him closer and closer to the edge only to back off and give him a minute. He wanted her to finish him, but he also wanted this to last as long as he could make it. He'd never been taken this way, and found that it was going to be one of his all-time favorite positions. When she lifted her head and looked at him, he could see her own hunger and need. And he wanted to satisfy her so much that he was ready to trade places with her. But she stepped back and stripped off her shirt.

"I want you to come down my throat. I want to feel your hot cum fill me." He nodded as her breasts swayed. She had no bra on, and when she lifted up her little skirt, he saw that she had no panties on, either.

"You planned this." She nodded. "You planned to seduce me in our kitchen. And I let you."

"Yes, you did. Now shut up and let me finish you." She licked the stream of precum off his cock, and he grabbed her head, lifted her up, and pulled her to his mouth. Kissing her hard, he held her tighter by twisting his hand harder in her hair.

"When I come down your throat, I want you to go to the table and lean over it. I'm going to fuck you hard and give you twice what you're doing to me." She licked her lips, and he watched her tongue. "You're playing with fire, Ally. Do you know that?"

"Yes." She jerked from him, wrapped her mouth over him, and swallowed. His cock exploded, his ball let go of his cum so hard and so quickly that he felt pain from it. Even as he roared, he felt her cup his balls and give them a gentle, but firm, squeeze. He came again, filling her as he emptied himself.

Jerking her off him again, she backed up. She reached for him, and he turned her and nearly tossed her across the table, her ass presented to him like an offering. He brought his hand down hard on the firm flesh and watched as his print pinkened up and made him want more.

"You were told to get into this position when I came, weren't you?" She didn't answer, but he knew that she was excited. Her entire body looked ready, ready for him. He reached around her and ran his fingers through her soaking curls and pinched her clit. She rocked into his hand, and he pulled away.

"Alistair, please." He slapped her ass again and heard her low moan. His cock stretched out before him like a beacon, and he pulled her hips back to him, but didn't enter her. She rode his cock as he played with her this way. When she laid her head down on the table, he spread her feet wider and leaned over her. His cock head was just at her entrance, and he knew that the moment he slammed into her they were both going to come.

"I'm not going to fuck you hard, Ally. I'm going to pull back, and you're going to lie over this table with your legs spread wide, and I'm going to eat you until I have my fill." She rocked back, and his cock slid more into her. "Then I'm going to fuck you. Fill your pussy with my cum until you can't take any more."

She nodded, and when he licked his way down her spine, he could taste how much she needed him. It poured from her body. When she sat on the table and lay back, he nearly changed his mind and took her then, but he pulled a chair in front of her and sat down. Christ, it was like a fucking feast.

Letting a little of his cat go, he felt his tongue elongate and knew that as soon as he entered her she was going to come for him. His cat snarled at him to get with it, and he leaned in and gave him what he wanted. She screamed so loudly that his cat snarled at her. Her cream dripped from her sheath, and he almost couldn't drink it all. Opening her wider for him, he suckled at her lips and nipped at them. She grabbed his hair and held him to her as she came again. This time when he nipped at her, he took her swollen clit into his mouth and pressed his thumb over her tiny rosette. She nearly knocked him away when she came this time, and he knew that he wasn't going to last much longer.

Wrapping his hand around his cock, he thought about coming this way while he finished her off. But he needed to mark her again if for no other reason than his cat was begging him to. When he stood up, he shoved the chair from under him and heard it crash against the counter as he filled her. Leaning over her, he nuzzled her throat and, without licking it to deaden some of the pain, he sank his teeth into her shoulder.

She gripped him hard, her legs tightened, her nails digging into his back. When he commanded her to come, she bowed up her body as tightly as a rubber band. And then she snapped. Her nails raked down his back, her heels plunging deep into his thighs. Even as he came again, he could feel her slipping away, her body going limp and her arms letting go.

When he spilled the last of his seed into her, he sealed off the ragged wound and leaned to her ear and whispered: "I love you more than I do myself. I want to grow old with you, showing you every day how much you mean to me, how much I love being with you. I want you swollen with our baby so that I can watch you grow our child. I love you, Allyson Golden, so much that I can't breathe through it."

She heard him. He knew when she smiled at him. Lifting his body from hers, he looked at what he'd done to her, and what she'd done to him. They had torn at each other. Her nails left long claw marks down his chest that were already healing. Bite marks marred his arms and shoulders. Her body looked the same, and blood stained her shoulder and breast where he'd bitten her. Smiling, he lifted her in his arms and took her to their bed. Gently laying her down, he covered her with the sheet and went downstairs to clean up. He laughed when he saw what he'd done to the chair.

It was shattered. His boxers hung from them limply, and his jeans were on the stove. He found his shirt in the sink over the tea glass from the night before. He picked up her things, as well. Her shirt was shredded, and it had somehow ended up across the room in front of the door; her skirt that he didn't even remember taking off her was under the table. He tossed them all in the trash, only to dig them out and take them to the bedroom.

Sliding into the bed with her, he pulled her into his arms and felt her wrap around him. Closing his eyes, he knew that they'd be lucky if they woke by nightfall. Shifting on the bed, he reached for Ryland.

"I won't be able to make it over today. At least not until much later. Ally and I have worked things out, and we're resting now." His brother laughed. *"I'm sorry."*

"I'm not. I'm glad. She was looking a little lost." His brother paused. *"When you come over, I have a couple of things I want to ask you. No biggy, but just wondering."*

He told him he'd be there late and closed the connection. He felt his mind drifting off when he thought of the chair again. Jed was not going to be amused. Then again, maybe he would.

~~~

"What do you mean I have to let the project go? There are things in here that could be a concern for our welfare as humans." His boss and a huge dick only shook his head. Sheldon wanted to stand up and knock him on his ass.

"You've been warned twice now that this information is to be put into storage and not to be bothered with again. Nor are you to speak of it to anyone in any way, shape, or form. Give it up, Peirce. It's nothing but the ramblings of the deluded mind of a drug addict."

As he walked away, Sheldon looked at what had become his obsession. There was some truth to this, and he knew it, and had a feeling the prick knew it as well. He stood up to start putting the things into the box when something slipped to the floor. It was a small sheet of paper with writing on it. He was just bending over to get it when he saw the man he worked for, Tony, coming back from lunch. He wondered if he had anything to do with him being pulled from this work when the man sat down and stared at him.

"I suppose the report you're supposed to write for our real work didn't get done." Sheldon tried to remember what it was he was supposed to have done. "I didn't think so. You have your head so far up your ass in this bullshit that you're going to lose your job if you don't give it up."

"There's enough stuff here that warrants looking into. The woman changed into a cat. Doesn't anyone think that's amazing?" Tony snorted. "I went to see his wife."

That brought Tony up short. He didn't move, but he could see that he wanted to bolt. They'd been told never to contact anyone they'd been hired to investigate, but seeing Mrs. Jane Cunningham had been a real eye opener.

"She said that she's met the woman. That she saw her change into a cat and that she'd put a hex on her." Sheldon didn't really believe that part, but he was beginning to see where the other just might be true. "Her name is—"

"I don't want to know," Tony said, cutting him off. "I don't ever want to know any of the shit you think you have on this case. And you're insane if you think that no one is ever going to find out you have been working on this instead of the other projects that come to us. I'm really getting tired of carrying your ass."

So he hadn't told them. Not yet, at any rate. Sheldon sat down and looked at the paper on the floor, and wondered if he should just leave it there or take it home with him. He had much more information there than here, anyway. He looked at Tony.

"You're right. I guess I've been a little nuts over this. But it's more interesting than some of the shit we've been getting in lately." Tony nodded and stood up when he did. "I'll box this crap up and have it stored away. Then I'll write that report."

"I wrote it already." But Sheldon had already figured that out and put his foot down over the paper on the floor as Tony began helping him put the stuff in the box. "And I'm glad you're doing this before it gets out of hand. You don't want to lose your job this late in our lives. It'll be a bitch trying to get another one that pays this well."

He was right, but that didn't make it any less boring. As soon as everything was put away, he and Tony loaded it on the cart they would use to lock away all their projects at the end of the day. He grinned to himself when he thought of the walls of information he had in his basement right now, and wondered what Tony would do if he saw that.

He knocked his pen to the floor and bent to get it and the piece of paper. He slipped it into his pocket along with his little note pad. He was just heading out anyway. and decided to read it in the car. As soon as he started his car, he pulled out the paper. It looked like a map address with longitude and latitude, and wondered where it was. He smiled, thinking of the fun he'd have when he started on this little bit of information.

"Bronwyn Lawrence, you're about to be in a world of hurt."

ABOUT THE AUTHOR

Kathi Barton, author of the bestselling series Force of Nature, lives in Nashport, Ohio with her husband Paul. In addition to writing full time Kathi likes to spend time with her eight grandkids, three children and three children-in-laws. She writes to relax and have fun.

Her muse, a cross between Jimmy Stewart and Hugh Jackman, brings them to life for her readers in a way that has them coming back time and again for more. Her favorite genre is paranormal romance with a great deal of spice. You can visit Kathi on line and drop her an email if you'd like. She loves hearing from her fans. aaronskiss@gmail.com.

Follow Kathi on her blog:
http://kathisbartonauthor.blogspot.com/

www.ingramcontent.com/pod-product-compliance
Lightning Source LLC
Chambersburg PA
CBHW030319180626
46810CB00003B/1158